# A CRY IN
# THE DARK

# Books by Beverly Lewis

## GIRLS ONLY (GO!)
### Youth Fiction

| | |
|---|---|
| *Dreams on Ice* | *Follow the Dream* |
| *Only the Best* | *Better Than Best* |
| *A Perfect Match* | *Photo Perfect* |
| *Reach for the Stars* | *Star Status* |

## SUMMERHILL SECRETS
### Youth Fiction

| | |
|---|---|
| *Whispers Down the Lane* | *House of Secrets* |
| *Secret in the Willows* | *Echoes in the Wind* |
| *Catch a Falling Star* | *Hide Behind the Moon* |
| *Night of the Fireflies* | *Windows on the Hill* |
| *A Cry in the Dark* | *Shadows Beyond the Gate* |

## HOLLY'S HEART
### Youth Fiction

| | |
|---|---|
| *Best Friend, Worst Enemy* | *Good-Bye, Dressel Hills* |
| *Secret Summer Dreams* | *Straight-A Teacher* |
| *Sealed With a Kiss* | *No Guys Pact* |
| *The Trouble With Weddings* | *Little White Lies* |
| *California Crazy* | *Freshman Frenzy* |
| *Second-Best Friend* | *Mystery Letters* |

*www.BeverlyLewis.com*

03B

SUMMERHILL SECRETS

# A CRY IN THE DARK

## Beverly Lewis

BETHANY HOUSE PUBLISHERS
MINNEAPOLIS, MINNESOTA 55438

*A Cry in the Dark*
Copyright © 1996
Beverly Lewis

Cover illustration by Chris Ellison

Published by Bethany House Publishers
11400 Hampshire Avenue South
Bloomington, Minnesota 55438
www.bethanyhouse.com

Bethany House Publishers is a Division of
Baker Book House Company, Grand Rapids, Michigan

Printed in the United States of America by
Bethany Press International, Bloomington, Minnesota 55438

**Library of Congress Cataloging-in-Publication Data**

Lewis, Beverly, 1949–
    A cry in the dark / by Beverly Lewis.
        p.  cm. — (SummerHill secrets ; 5)
    Summary: After praying for God to fill the hole in her life left by the death of her twin sister, thirteen-year-old Merry finds an abandoned baby outside her house.
    ISBN 1-55661-480-2
    [1. Abandoned children—Fiction.  2. Babies—Fiction.
3. Sisters—Fiction.  4. Christian life—Fiction.]  I. Title.
II. Series: Lewis, Beverly, 1949–     SummerHill secrets ; 5.
PZ7.L58464Crn    1996
[Fic]—dc20
                                   96–4445
                                     CIP
                                     AC

For
Barb Lilland,
who first shared the dream
that became
SummerHill Secrets.
And . . .
who received
a true gift from God
on
Christmas Eve 1995—
Jordan Robert.

BEVERLY LEWIS is a speaker, teacher, and the best-selling author of the HOLLY'S HEART series. She has written more than thirty books for teens and children. Many of her articles and stories have appeared in the nation's top magazines.

Beverly is a member of The National League of American Pen Women, the Society of Children's Book Writers and Illustrators, and Colorado Christian Communicators. She and her husband, Dave, along with their three teenagers, live in Colorado. She fondly remembers their cockapoo named Cuddles, who used to snore to Mozart!

A joy that's shared is
a joy made double.

—Anonymous

# ONE

"Don't move!" I aimed my camera lens at the blond, wispy-haired girl posing on my front porch. "This is it! A truly amazing shot. Don't breathe!"

"For how long?" Lissa Vyner asked, smiling.

"Till I say so."

Slowly, I backed away from the porch, where my friend balanced gracefully on the white banister leading to the sidewalk. Dressed in summer pink, she put on airs for the camera. She'd worn the dazzling junior brides-maid's dress to her cousin's wedding last week, and by the dreamy look on her face, I knew she was still chock-full of romantic whimsy.

Three more shots. Each took several minutes to set up. That's how I liked to work—meticulously. Photography was my passion.

"Hurry, Merry, it's hot out here," Lissa urged.

"Can't rush a masterpiece." I carefully checked the aperture on my camera, adjusting the lens opening for appropriate light.

Out of the corner of my eye, I noticed a pickup truck coming down SummerHill Lane. The noisy muffler captured my curiosity. I wouldn't have bothered to look, except the old rattletrap swerved off the road, crept along the shoulder, and came to a shuddering stop right in front of our mailbox.

"Expecting company?" Lissa teased.

I had no idea who the driver was or what he wanted. And since my parents were in Lancaster running errands, I kept my distance.

A hefty guy in his early twenties leaned his arm on the window and hollered out, "Ya'll live here?" He glanced for a moment at Lissa, who was still perched on the banister waiting for the next picture.

"Are you lost?" I asked, avoiding his question.

"Jist wonderin' about this here neck of the woods" came the reply. "Shore would call it the sticks back home. Not much activity round." His eyes were a hot blue—far different from the kind, innocent blue of Lissa's eyes. I felt uneasy.

"Are you looking for a street address?" I asked politely, careful not to display my concern.

"No, ma'am, I ain't." His accent was southern, and his answer rather blunt. He ran a chapped hand through his thick, greasy hair. "Is thar a doctor in these here parts?"

"Is someone sick?" I studied him from my vantage point. He didn't appear to be in need of medical help.

"Well, it ain't yer run-of-the-mill sickness, if that's whatcha mean. . . ." His voice trailed off.

"There's a hospital in town about twenty minutes away." Although our mailbox noted the fact that my dad was an ER doctor, I was hesitant to divulge family information, especially to a stranger.

"In town, ya say?" He craned his neck, looking around. "Alls I see is fields and barns, and . . ." He paused. "Them plain folks . . . uh, whatcha call 'em?"

"They're Pennsylvania Amish." I said it proudly, as though I were one of them. My great-great-grandfather had been Amish, and one of my dearest friends, Rachel Zook down the lane, was, too.

The stranger nodded, scratching his left eyebrow. "Well, thanks for yer help. I speck I best be goin'." With that, he turned on the ignition and steered his clunky pickup onto the road and down the hill.

I scurried up the lawn to Lissa. "Did you catch that?"

She nodded. "Seemed kinda strange."

"Sure did," I said, fooling with my camera. "I'm glad he's gone."

Lissa agreed. "Did you notice his license plate?"

"Nope, did you?"

"Well, I know it wasn't a Pennsylvania plate, but I couldn't see the state." She wiggled around, swinging her legs. "How much longer do I have to sit here?"

"Just keep smiling. I'm almost done—honest." *Click!* I took five more shots before calling it quits. "Okay, you can relax now," I said, walking toward her.

"Grammy will be so thrilled." She stood up and brushed herself off.

"Why'd your grandma want so many pictures?" I leaned against the porch railing.

"Grammy Vyner broke her hip last week and couldn't come to my cousin's wedding," Lissa explained. "You should meet her sometime, Merry. My grammy lives for family events. Her life revolves around them." She sighed. "Her hip surgery—the whole thing—completely devastated her."

"She probably wanted to see her granddaughter in a dress, right?" I laughed.

"Silly you." Lissa swirled around, and the long, fancy skirt billowed out. "It's not like I never wear one."

I put my camera in its case and set it down on the step. "Okay, when was the last time, not counting the wedding?"

Lissa stared at the cornfield across the lane. "Let's see . . ."

I waited, then—"See! You can't remember the last time you had on a dress."

"Merry Hanson, don't exaggerate!" She chased after me as I ran down the sloping front yard toward the dirt road.

"When's the last time you ran in dress shoes?" I yelled back.

But my taunting didn't stop Lissa. She kicked off her white patent-leather pumps and ran along the road in her nylons through the wild strawberry vines nestled in the grassy ditch.

"Watch out for garter snakes," I teased.

"What?" She stopped running.

I turned around, calling back to her. "Didn'tcha know? Snakes come out when city girls come to visit."

"Merry!" she hollered. "You know that's not one bit true! Besides, I'm *not* a city girl!"

I grinned at her, my good friend Lissa Vyner. Gullible. Stubborn too. Pete's sake, she'd stolen Jon Klein, my secret love, out from under my nose. But that had been last spring. Lissa and Jon were a thing of the past.

"Thirsty?" I asked.

She wiped the perspiration off her face. "It's way too hot, running around in this heat."

"Okay, we'll go inside and cool off." I hurried up the lane, matching her stride. "The humidity's a killer."

We walked up the hill together, past the willow grove and the shortcut to the Zooks' farm. Then I heard a familiar noise. The sound of that rickety old pickup. It was coming up the lane, right behind us!

"Look who's back," Lissa said as the truck slowed down.

"Let's go!" I grabbed her arm, and we ran all the way up the hill to my house. When we were safely inside, I peeked through the living-room curtains, catching my breath.

"What's he want?" Lissa whispered.

"I wish I knew."

The two of us watched as the faded pickup slowed to a crawl. The driver eyeballed the house. My heart pounded when his eyes came to rest on our mailbox. "Oh no," I whispered. "Now he knows Dad's a doctor. What if he comes to the door?"

"It's locked, right?" Lissa asked softly.

I nodded. Still, I was fearful.

Then, without warning, the faded blue truck accelerated, struggling against the steep grade. It snorted and puffed, leaving a trail of dust in its path.

"Man, he needs some new wheels," Lissa remarked, a hint of relief in her voice.

"A new muffler, too," I said, remembering what my older brother had told me about worn-out mufflers. For once, something Skip had said actually stuck in my brain.

"That guy scares me," Lissa said, still peering out the window. "What's he want?"

"I know one thing, I wasn't going to stick around to find out."

"Maybe he's a serial killer," she suggested.

"We're still alive, aren't we?" I forced a laugh, which helped lessen the tension. "There's something weird about it, though. Something about the way he kept checking the place out. And looking at our mailbox."

"What could it mean?"

"I'm not sure," I said. "I hope he's not a burglar."

Lissa and I headed up the long wooden staircase to the second story of my family's hundred-year-old farm-house.

"I can't wait to put on some jeans," she said as we entered my room.

"See, I told you! You hate dresses." We laughed about it. I'd caught her good.

While Lissa changed clothes, I put my camera away, trying to shake off the weird feeling. But as hard as I tried, I couldn't get the stranger in the blue pickup out of my mind. I must admit—he gave me the willies!

# TWO

"It's a scorcher," Dad said as he and Mom came into the kitchen loaded with grocery bags.

"You're tellin' me." I got up to help. "It was so hot, Mrs. Vyner brought ice cream over when she came to pick up Lissa. The three of us made cones and sat out in the gazebo trying to cool off."

Mom turned the lazy susan in the corner of one kitchen cabinet. "How's Lissa doing these days?"

I knew she really wanted to know how Lissa's *father* was doing. He'd had severe problems with alcohol and abuse—so bad that Lissa had run away. Thankfully, those frightening days were behind them. "Lissa says things are totally different since her dad's been going for therapy."

"So, you think the abuse has stopped?" Mom asked, searching me with all-knowing brown eyes.

"I'm one-hundred-percent-amen sure."

Mom smiled. "That's good."

I stretched on tiptoes, sliding two cans of tuna onto the top corner shelf. "Lissa says her mom's going to invite him to the church potluck next week."

"Great idea," she said. "I hope he'll come."

I smiled, watching Mom dash around the kitchen, putting things away. The old tension-filled days between us were gone. Mom was relaxed now, no longer preoccupied with the loss of Faithie—my twin sister—who had died of cancer the summer she was seven. Actually, Mom's cheerful demeanor surprised me because the anniversary of Faithie's death was coming up. Three days from now—July thirty-first.

Dad hauled in two more grocery sacks before sitting down with a glass of iced tea. "Sure will be nice to have your brother home," he remarked to me.

My obnoxious big brother had gone to help out at a camp for handicapped kids—something he did every summer. This time would be his last before heading off to college next month. I couldn't wait for that moment. Total peace and quiet—my life could possibly be stress-free for a change. "When's Skip supposed to get back?" I asked.

"Let's see." Dad pulled a pocket calendar from his wallet. "He'll be home the weekend after next."

"Just in time for the church potluck," Mom added happily. My parents missed their one-and-only son. That was plain to see. Losing their firstborn to college would be tough.

"Need some sugar?" I asked Dad, bringing over the bowl and setting it near his glass.

He waved his hand. "Nah, I'm cutting back on sweets all around."

"Hey, that's a first," I teased.

"Your father's counting calories these days," Mom

said, coming over to sit at the table. "He'll be fifty next month, you know."

*Fifty in August,* I thought. Someone else was having a birthday next month. His seventeenth. But I didn't want to clutter my brain with Levi Zook just now. Rachel Zook's brother had shocked the local Amish community and decided to go off to a Mennonite Bible school. Oh, sure, he and I were still friends—very good friends, in fact—but I hadn't exactly thought through a possible long-distance relationship. Levi hadn't either.

Besides, now that Jon Klein was available . . . well, I wanted to wait and see what might happen.

                 ❧     ❧

Later, during supper, I brought up the subject of the stranger. "Have you ever seen an old blue pickup around here? The jalopy has a really bad muffler."

Mom shook her head. "Why do you ask?"

"Just wondered," I said. "The driver seems displaced, I guess."

"Homeless, perhaps?" Dad suggested.

"I don't think so. It's hard to put a finger on it," I said, "but I know there's something truly strange going on."

"Well," Dad said, rubbing his hands together, "I'll be on the lookout. In the meantime, keep the doors and windows locked at night, okay?"

I must admit I was glad our bedrooms were high up on the second floor. Without air-conditioning, it was way too hot to sleep with the bedroom windows closed. Around here, we called these sultry summer days, dog days. Even the dogs were hot. Cats too.

Mom pinched off the dead blooms on her African violets while I loaded the dishwasher. She had a knack for making them flourish—even the velvety green leaves looked plump. Her plants dazzled the corner of our country kitchen with blossoms of purple, pink, and snowy white.

"Do you think Dad has an enemy?" I said, letting the words slip out.

Mom straightened up and turned to look at me. "Honey, why would you think such a thing?"

It was the stranger. I couldn't get him out of my mind. I folded the dishcloth before responding. "It just seems weird that a guy would be asking around for a doctor, like maybe he was trying to track dad down or something."

"It's most likely a simple coincidence," Mom offered, going back to violet pinching.

"Maybe." I left the kitchen with Mom still fussing over her plant babies.

Upstairs, I grew more and more impatient with the stifling heat. It was too hot for a shower up here, I decided. So I went to my room and found clean clothes, a bath towel, and a brush for my hair.

I dashed down the steep back steps leading to the kitchen and flicked on the light as I opened the door leading to the basement. Dad had rigged up a small shower in our cellar years before, but we rarely used it. My cats, Shadrach, Meshach, and Abednego followed close behind. Lily White, my kitten, was probably outside snoozing under the gazebo.

Musty and cool, the cellar was a welcome change in temperature, and I congratulated myself on this wise

18

move. I ran the water, making it tepid, the perfect temperature to refresh my perspiring body. While scrubbing my arms, I thought of Faithie. She'd hated this dark cellar—in fact, she had recoiled at anything related to darkness. I remembered several moonless nights long ago when she had crawled into bed with me, trembling with fear.

*Poor little Faithie,* I thought.

I missed her terribly. In all my nearly fourteen years, no one had come along to truly soothe the pain of loss. No one. And yet I longed for it. Prayed for it.

It wasn't like I didn't have good friends. I had plenty of them at school and at church. And there was always Rachel Zook, my Amish girlfriend in the farmhouse beyond the willows. Her youngest sister, Susie, and I had become close pals, too. But something always seemed unsettled—amiss—in the soul of me. I longed for a Faithie replacement. Someone just like her.

I reached up and turned the cold spigot just enough to cool the water, letting it beat on my back. Then I began to pray. "Dear Lord, it's been such a long time since I mentioned this, but maybe you could find it in your will to help me. I feel sad, like I haven't in a long time. Maybe it's because of July thirty-first . . . it's coming so soon. Faithie's gone-to-heaven day."

The memory made my heart heavy, and tears spilled down my face. Purposefully, I turned and raised my face toward the splashing stream, letting the water bounce off my cheeks. In that moment, I comforted myself with the knowledge that Faithie was surrounded by light. By Jesus himself! Never again to experience darkness or the fear of it.

"Oh, Lord," I cried. "Let some of that same light pour into my own heart."

I lingered in the shower stall long after I wrapped myself in a heavy towel, hoping for an answer.

# THREE

Hours later, as dusk approached, I sat outside in the gazebo. Wearing a long T-shirt and gray nylon jogging shorts, I relished the evening breeze. My cats, all four of them, surrounded me with their purring, cuddly selves.

"You guys weren't even born back when my twin sister was alive," I told them.

Abednego, the oldest, lifted his head nonchalantly as if to say, *I've heard this story before, thank you kindly.*

"Don't give me that look," I reprimanded. "You should be thankful I took you and your brothers in. Homeless strays, that's what you were."

Lily White shook her head and a dainty little sneeze flew out. Shadrach pounced on her, and off they went, down the white gazebo steps, rolling and playing. Meshach eventually got in on the action, but it was Abednego who stayed closest to me. Usually, *he* was the one off somewhere else.

"What's the matter, little boy?" I touched his soft black head. "Too tired to play?"

He twitched his whiskers.

"Are you protecting your mistress Merry?" I chuckled, thinking of Jon Klein. He'd often referred to me as Mistress Merry, a direct result of our private alliteration word game.

Jon and his family were off on a camping trip in the Poconos. The Alliteration Wizard had actually called to say goodbye. The old spark was definitely alive between us.

Lissa, of course, knew nothing of it. She'd had her chance with Jon, and although they seemed to get along fine, I knew she wasn't a candidate for alliteration competition. Not to boast, but for as long as I'd known Jon, he and I had had this amazing attraction to word play. Because of it, we were drawn to each other.

*Merry, Mistress of Mirth* was Jon's favorite way to address me. He was an intelligent, jovial guy, but totally spacey when it came to girls. I often wondered if he had any idea how I felt about him. Jon head-in-the-clouds Klein was special in more ways than one. He was one of the few friends I had who'd actually known Faithie—besides Rachel and Levi Zook and their family, of course, and a friend from school named Chelsea Davis.

"Merry!" My mom's voice jolted me back. "Someone's on the phone for you."

"Coming." I got up and hurried toward the back door. Abednego followed close behind. I held the screen door for him, then hurried to the phone. "Hello?"

"Hullo, Merry. It's Levi. I'm calling from town."

"Hi. What's up?"

He paused, probably getting up the nerve to ask me out. "Uh . . . Merry, how would ya like to go to a concert with me next Saturday night?"

"Saturday?"

"*Jah,* in Ephrata at a Mennonite church."

It sounded like fun, but we were planning to attend our church potluck that same afternoon, and family church events often spilled over into the evening. Besides, Jon Klein would be back from camping, and I wanted to see him. "I hope you didn't buy the tickets yet," I said.

"Jah, I did. Just hopin'—ya know." There was an eager, almost impatient tone to his voice.

"Well, I can't go," I said. "I'm sorry."

"*Ach,* Merry, won'tcha think about it?" Now I knew he was perturbed.

"Please don't push me," I retorted.

"Merry? Is something wrong?"

I sighed. "I'm having a rough day."

His voice grew softer. "I could come over and we could talk." His gentle words tugged at me.

"Thanks, but I'm really tired."

"Oh." He sounded dejected. "Maybe if—"

"Not tonight," I said, wishing things hadn't been left hanging between Levi and me.

"Okay, then. I'll talk to ya soon, Merry."

"Goodbye." I must've been in a fog standing there holding the phone because Mom waved her hand in front of my face. "Mer? Everything okay?" she whispered.

I exhaled and hung up the phone. I needed to talk to someone. Was Mom a good choice? Would she understand my frustration—being caught between *two* boys?

I pulled my hair back into a ponytail and then freed it, studying her. "Mom? Can we go somewhere private?"

Her face broke into a full smile. "You name the place."

"Ever been to the willow grove?" I asked sheepishly.

"Oh . . . the secret place?"

I grinned. "How do you know about that?"

We were already walking toward the back door. "Faithie took me there once," she confessed.

"Faithie?" I was baffled. The secret place had always been off limits to adults. Always. It was one of those special spots that existed in the heart or the imagination— but had the uncanny benefit of being *real*.

"She took me there several weeks before she died," Mom admitted, her eyes still shining.

Once again, Faithie had beat me to the punch. She had always been an expert at it—loved being the first to show Mom things. Schoolwork, her drawings . . . everything. Maybe her need to do that came from having been the firstborn twin by about twenty minutes. I felt a twinge of resentment.

"Are you sure you want to go to the willows?" Mom asked.

"I'm sure." I led the way outside through the backyard and around the long side yard, to the dirt road which was SummerHill Lane. Reaching up, I caught a firefly. "It's been a long time since we really talked," I began.

"And I take all the blame for that," she said.

"You?"

She nodded. "Up until a few weeks ago, I couldn't bring myself to this point. But now . . ." She stopped. "Of course, that has nothing to do with you. Anyway, I'm very sorry."

24

Mom turned at the shortcut to the willows as though she'd been here more than once. I wondered but followed in silence. The path was only wide enough for walking single file, worn from constant use. Rachel and I met often in the secret place. Six-year-old Susie, too. Levi and I had never come here, however. Nor Jon. It was a leafy green haven for the kid in you, not a romantic hideaway.

At last we found it, the secluded place—encircled by wispy willow tendrils, some thicker than others, and cushioned by the soft grassy floor beneath the arms of graceful branches. Fireflies were thick with light, creating a magical atmosphere.

"Just coming here helps sometimes," I said.

"I know." Mom brushed the hair away from her face.

"You've been here since coming with Faithie the first time, haven't you, Mom?"

She nodded. "You're a perceptive girl, Merry. Much like your father."

"And Faithie was like you." It was a statement, not a question.

"I guess you could say there was a similarity."

"She even looked like you," I added.

Mom was quiet now. I studied her in the dim light of dusk, wishing she'd talk more freely.

"Did you ever think you were in love with two boys at once?" The question leaped off my lips.

She leaned back, looking at the sky. "There were two boys in my life when I was in high school. I can't say that I *loved* them both."

"What did you do?" I asked. "How did you decide?"

"I prayed about it."

Her spiritual approach didn't surprise me. "Tell me about it," I said, sitting on my knees.

"Well, my mother—your grandmother—told me once that she'd started praying for the man I would marry when I was just a toddler."

"Wow." This was truly amazing.

"And God arranged everything, right down to the fact that one of those boys started dating another girl his senior year. Of course, I felt that I'd lost a friend, but not my *best* friend—the other boy—who turned out to be your father."

"Really? Dad was one of the two guys?"

"Are you surprised?"

"So you're saying you might've ended up with someone other than Dad if you hadn't prayed?"

She looked at me as she spoke. "All three of us were Christians; we all wanted God's will for our lives. Both boys were perfectly suitable mates"—and here she laughed—"you get to know that by being good friends, by not being in a hurry. The Lord has a way of making things very clear."

I thought about what she'd said. Jon, Levi, and I were good friends, too. None of us was in a hurry. But perfectly suitable mates? I had no idea about either one. Not yet. Things weren't clear at all.

I wondered if Mom would start her you're-too-young-to-be-thinking-this-way-about-boys speech, but she didn't. We sat there enjoying the early evening. Together. Mother and daughter.

A gentle wind whispered through the willows, and I had a strange feeling. A feeling that the secret place would never be quite the same.

# FOUR

It was nearly eight when Mom and I returned to the house. She went into the family room where Dad had closed things up and turned on the only air-conditioner in the house. I said good-night and headed upstairs with my cats.

The second floor was sweltering. First thing, I opened all the windows in my room. Then I stood looking out across the expanse of field and sky. I hugged myself for a moment, thinking. The chat with Mom had warmed my heart. Was it a new beginning for us?

With July thirty-first so near, I knew I shouldn't hold my breath about it. Faithie's death had muddled things up—for nearly the last seven years. Especially between Mom and me. I could only hope that we'd made a breakthrough today in the willow grove. I decided to pray about it.

While I stared out the window, telling God my concerns, I heard a sound. In the distance, but coming closer. The cats raised their heads, cocking their ears. "It's the jalopy again," I whispered. "I'd recognize that bad muffler anywhere."

I waited behind the window curtains, watching. Then I saw it—the old blue pickup. It stopped in front of the house. My heart pounded.

I could see the stranger sitting in the driver's seat. This time someone was with him. A young woman. No . . . a young girl. Not much older than seventeen, if that.

Then I heard voices. Angry voices.

Shouting. Arguing.

I listened intently, trying to sort out what was being said.

"Go on—do it!" the man ordered.

The girl began to cry. Sad, horrible sobs. She got out of the truck and began to wring her hands in despair, looking into the cab of the truck every so often as though she were checking on something.

The man held up a bundle of laundry. "Do what I told ya!" he demanded.

The girl's voice was muffled with tears. "Please . . . no!"

"We haven't any choice, ya hear?" came the harsh reply.

"But I cain't . . . I cain't." More heart-wrenching sobs.

The man put down the dirty clothes and leaped out of the truck. He ran around the front of the pickup and grabbed hold of the girl, shaking her. "Now ya listen here, and ya listen good!"

I'd had enough. I couldn't stand by and watch this guy get brutal. I ran out of my room and down the front steps. Hesitating in the entryway, I wondered if I should get Dad to come out with me.

"Dad!" I called. "Come here!" Then I remembered. The air-conditioner was going full blast in the family room. No way could he hear me.

I dashed down the hall to the kitchen and out to the family room addition. I opened the door and peeked in. Dad was resting against the back of the recliner, sawing logs. Mom was nowhere in sight. She was probably in the shower upstairs, getting ready for bed.

I reached out to touch Dad. Lightly, I tapped his arm. He moved in his sleep just slightly. I realized he was out, and probably would be too hazy to help even if he did wake up.

Then and there, I decided I couldn't waste another minute. I turned and ran all the way down the front hallway. The screen door was locked, and I fumbled with the latch for several frantic seconds. Finally, when I got it open, I burst out of the house.

Standing on the porch, I scanned the road where just minutes before there'd been a battle raging. I couldn't believe my eyes. The pickup was gone. Vanished!

"Where'd they go?" Undaunted, I walked around the side yard facing Strawberry Lane.

No pickup and no girl.

Then I hurried around the front to the opposite side yard, facing the willow grove.

Nothing!

I leaned on a giant split log on the woodpile, puzzled. Hadn't I just witnessed a major fight? And what had that horrible guy been saying? I thought back to the frightening conversation. *Do what I told you!*

What did it mean? Was the girl the sick one? Was she

too shy to ring our doorbell—to talk to a doctor? Was that it?

I ran out to SummerHill Lane where the pickup truck had been parked, scouring the area. I searched the side of the road, in the grass, and near the mailbox. There was nothing to be found.

I looked in both directions, up the hill toward Strawberry Lane as far as I could see in the early moonlight, and all the way down, toward the Zooks' farm. Way in the distance, there appeared to be a tuft of smoke on the road, but I couldn't be sure.

*How'd they get away so fast?* I wondered. *And why?*

I was heading back around the side yard toward the gazebo when I heard another sound. The sound of a kitten fussing.

"Lily White, is that you?" I called. "Here, kitty kitty." I waited for Lily to come strutting her regal white self, but seconds passed and she didn't come.

Then I heard it again. This time louder. It didn't exactly sound like a kitten now, although with all that had just happened, maybe I was too shaken to sort it out.

I searched the area around me, listening, following the sound. "Lily?" I called again, beginning to worry that she'd gotten herself caught somewhere. I turned to look toward the willow grove, but it was getting too dark to determine anything without a flashlight. "Lily, are you stuck?"

The cry came again. And I began to realize it was not coming from the willows. The sound was coming from the backyard. From the gazebo.

I rushed to the white-latticed outdoor room. Inside, I

noticed a pile of clothes. My throat turned dry. *Weren't these the same ones I'd seen in the pickup—in the stranger's hands?*

Now they were all bunched up in the corner. Yet the sound came from inside the heap of clothes. Cautiously, I approached the mass of laundry, or what I thought to be clothes, and when I focused my eyes in the darkness, I realized these were blankets.

Then, I heard a distinct cry and curiously lifted the blankets. "What on earth?" I whispered into the night.

There, in a wicker laundry basket, was a baby!

I reached out in amazement and touched the thin, pink blanket. The small bundle moved slightly under my touch and began to whimper. "Oh, don't cry," I said, finding my voice. "It's okay." But I knew it wasn't.

I looked around, wondering if someone was hiding out in the darkness. Was this some kind of crazy joke?

*Wait a minute,* I thought. *Those people . . . those horrible people. Did they do this? Did they abandon this beautiful baby girl?*

I stood up and found the tin filled with matches and lit a citronella candle. "There. Now we can see better, can't we?" I said as much to the little one as to the dusk.

The baby cooed a sweet response, and the sound broke my heart. As I came back to kneel at the foot of the wicker basket, I noticed something. Something I'd missed before. A note pinned to the blanket.

Quickly, I removed the safety pin. And holding the note up to the candle, I began to read.

# FIVE

*To the finder: I am two months old. My bottle is in the basket. Please take care of me and love me as your own.*

I smoothed the paper and read the words again. *Love me as your own. . . .*

I hid the note in the basket and leaned close to the infant girl snuggled inside. Her eyes were closed, and her tiny face was wrapped in an angelic glow.

"You're beautiful," I whispered, stroking the satiny cheek. "I will take good care of you. I promise."

Gently, I searched the basket for a bottle. Babies needed bottles every few hours. I knew that because my twin cousins seemed to be hungry all the time.

Deep in the basket, I found an eight-ounce bottle filled with milk. The nipple had a plastic cap, and there were several cans of formula and some disposable diapers, too.

"Well, looks like someone planned ahead," I mumbled. But I was worried. Had the baby's parents truly abandoned her? And if so, why?

The idea of leaving a baby outside alone, even on a warm summer night, angered me. What were they thinking? I sat next to the wicker basket, never taking my eyes off the pink cheeks and the rosebud lips. "You're the most beautiful baby I've ever seen," I whispered. The lump in my throat grew bigger, and I thought I would cry. "How could they leave you?"

Tears sprang up and I let them fall. Silently, I cried for the baby nobody wanted. And I prayed. "Dear Lord, please help me take care of her. This darling little gift."

I stopped praying and clutched my aching throat. *A gift! Was the baby truly a gift from God . . . to me?*

My prayer!

Suddenly, I remembered. I'd prayed a prayer this very day—in the dank, dark cellar where I'd taken a shower to cool off. What exactly had I said to God?

I pondered my words. *What* had I prayed? Something about finding it in His will to help me. I hadn't specifically asked for a person—certainly not a baby—to fill the hole that Faithie's death had left in me. But now that this incredibly marvelous baby was here, I was beginning to wonder.

The light from the candle on the table cast a soft pink glow on the sleeping infant. She stirred peacefully, and as I watched, something in me longed to hold her. Strong feelings of responsibility and of love sprang up in me. I'd never felt like this about a baby. Typically, babies scared me to pieces, made me uncomfortable. When they first had come for a visit, even my baby cousins Ben and Becky made me nervous.

I gazed at the baby in her wicker bed. She was different somehow. "Let's make sure you're all right," I said, reaching into the basket.

I brought her up into my arms. She lifted her tiny fist and waved it in the air. I put my finger next to the plump little hand, and she grabbed hold with a mighty grip. Slowly, I carried her to the table, where the citronella candle sent out its rosy glow. I wanted to get a better look at the sleepy bundle.

There in the candlelight, I pulled back her limp blanket and saw only the lightweight cotton undershirt and diaper she wore. I placed my hand on the soft chest and tummy.

"I think it's time to give you a name," I said. "I'll name you Charity. Baby Charity."

My words, the loudest I'd spoken, must've startled her because she opened her eyes. I looked down into the bluest eyes I'd ever seen. As blue as the heavens. Charity squinted at the candlelight as if to say: *I'm trying to say hello, but it's too bright.*

I wrapped the pink blanket around her again and picked her up, moving back into the shadows of the gazebo, away from the light. "Do you like your name?" I whispered, almost cooing as I spoke to her. "It fits you." I sighed. "You don't know it, but I had a twin sister named Faith. I think she would be very happy to know that you've come to me." Again the tears fell, dripping off my chin onto Charity's baby blanket.

Now that she was here—this amazing gift from God—what was I going to do with her? I was sure Mom and Dad had already retired for the night. A quick glance at the house confirmed that. Mom probably thought I'd already gone to bed. And Dad? Well, he'd been zonked out earlier. I envisioned him stumbling up the back steps to bed, exhausted as usual.

For several years now, I'd gone to bed on my own without the old childhood tucking-in ritual. I think it was Mom's way of letting me grow up, spread my wings. Although, if I'd been honest, I would've told her I missed it—being covered up and kissed good-night.

I leaned down and kissed Charity's soft forehead. "I know what we'll do. We'll sleep outside together, right here. It's a nice, warm night, and this way, you won't wake up my parents. They don't need to know about you just yet." I wanted to savor this precious moment—my special time with Charity—just the two of us. Before anyone else found out. At least for tonight, she belonged to me.

I kept talking softly to her, the way I did to my cats, who by now were probably sacked out on my bed. "We'll sleep together here in the gazebo, over in the corner just like Faithie and I did once." I caught myself before I said more. But I couldn't stop the memory.

That splendid night was as clear as though it were yesterday. It had been one short month before Faithie died. She'd begged to sleep out under the stars in the gazebo. We were really young—seven, going on eight, but surprisingly, Mom and Dad had agreed. They'd left their windows wide open. Just in case we needed something.

Thinking back, I was sure it was a granting of a "last wish." My parents knew Faithie was dying, and she could be mighty determined sometimes.

Rachel Zook had joined us that night. She was only eight and a half, but seemed lots older than Faithie and me. Rachel's mother, however, had insisted that she bring along her pony and tie him to the gazebo railing—to alert us if there were strangers lurking. But we never feared. Barely slept, either. We were three kids having a good time. One of the last good times before . . .

All of it came rushing back. The sweet, fresh smell of honeysuckle filling the air. And the fireflies. Trillions of them.

I cuddled Charity next to me and felt the steady rising and falling of her breathing. She felt good in my arms. I wanted to hold her forever.

All around were blinking fireflies. And the fragrant aroma of honeysuckle. The air was thick with summer sounds and smells. Charity sighed in her sleep the way Faithie often did.

It was as though time had flip-flopped.

## SIX

Baby Charity soon became restless. Instead of waiting for her to cut loose with the demanding cries of a hungry baby, I offered her the lukewarm milk in the bottle. She was more than willing to take it and made the gurgling, contented sounds of eager sucking.

When the milk was half gone and she was slowing down a bit, I put her up on my shoulder the way I'd seen Aunt Teri do it. Charity let out a few resounding burps and cooed a bit, then seemed fussy again.

"You're still hungry, aren't you, sweetie?" I turned her around and placed her in my arms, offering her the bottle again. While she drank, I pretended she was my own baby, singing softly the way a real mother would.

My thoughts drifted to Charity's mother, wherever she was. Had she been the young girl—the teenager—I'd seen in front of the house? Was she being forced to give up her baby?

Shivering, I remembered the frightening incident which had brought me outside in the first place. The girl had needed help, that was evident. She'd pleaded with the man in the driver's seat. Sobbed pitifully. But the man in the blue pickup was relentless. Who *was* he? Certainly not the father of this baby. This wonderful baby!

I glanced down at Charity, now sound asleep. She was so helpless—no parents. No mother to care for her. I touched the top of her head where her light brown hair formed tiny ringlets. *I* was the one Charity needed. A girl like me would never let her down. Never!

Yet two sides were arguing inside my head.

*I found her! She's mine!* the selfish, dreamy side insisted.

*You're just a kid yourself,* the opposite side reasoned. *You can't take care of a baby!*

My heart pounded ninety miles an hour, and eventually the selfish side of me won out. I put Charity back into her basket. Certain that she was in a deep sleep, I hurried to get the pad off the new chaise lounge in the yard. It would be my bed for the night. As for a cover, the night was still warm, but I borrowed one of the lightweight blankets left behind with Charity.

Peacefully, we settled down in our enchanting gazebo house. I situated her in the most well-protected corner and lay beside her, watching her in the moonlight. Minutes later, I gave in to droopy eyes.

My sleep was sweet, filled with a glorious dream. A wonderful voice said, "Your prayer has been answered, Merry Hanson."

In the recesses of my mind, I knew God had given this new baby sister to me. Dream or no dream!

✣  ✣

I awakened with a start. The sun was just peeking over

the horizon as I leaned up to look at Charity. Her little fist was moving as she peeped her eyes open.

There were sounds of *clip-clopping* as a horse and buggy made its way down SummerHill Lane. I wondered if Rachel would be going to market with her mother. It was Friday, and lots of plain folk would be in downtown Lancaster at Central Market, tending their fruit stands and selling quilts and other handmade things to tourists.

"We've got to have a talk," I said to the baby. "You need some clothes—and that's not all. This basket bed you're sleeping in is going to get very small pretty soon."

She gurgled and smiled in response. Such a happy, contented baby! I continued our chat, locating a disposable diaper in the basket, careful not to lose the note from Charity's mother, or whoever had written it.

Suddenly, I realized someone was watching us!

I spun around. Rachel Zook peered into the gazebo. "Ach, Merry. Who're ya talkin' to?"

I noticed her brown work dress and long, black apron. She'd already been out milking. "What are you doing over here at the crack of dawn?"

Rachel spied the baby. "What a perty baby. Whose is it?"

"It's too long a story for now," I said. "Just promise me something."

She smoothed the hair under her prayer *kapp* before she spoke again. "Promise ya what?"

"That you won't tell a single soul about this." Desperation seized me.

Rachel's blue eyes widened, and she crept closer. "I

don't know. . . ." She paused, frowning. "Where'd the baby come from?"

I didn't dare tell Rachel the whole story—not even one smidgen of it. She'd go running off to tell her mother, and before I'd know it, my secret would be out. And my plan ruined.

"Who is she, then?" Rachel asked.

"Her name is Charity." I hoped that was enough to quiet my friend.

"Charity what?"

"I don't need an interrogation," I said.

Her jaw dropped. "I didn't mean to upset ya. I just came over to see if you was up yet."

"What for?"

"Levi wants to talk to ya." She tried to keep a straight face, but a tiny smirk crossed her lips.

"Well, I can't leave Charity alone, so tell him maybe later."

Rachel put her hand on my shoulder. "What's goin' on, really? This baby . . . uh, Merry, why don't ya just tell me about it?"

"Tell you what?" She'd known me too long. Close friends could pick up on unspoken things easily.

"You're bein' too secretive for this not to be what I'm a-thinkin'." Rachel knelt down beside me. "Let's take her over to the farm. *Mam* will know what to do."

I bristled. "This is something *I* have to do."

"Mam's raisin' seven of us children, Merry." My friend wasn't usually this determined. Amish girls were taught to be yielding and compliant.

"Just because your mom's got a bunch of kids doesn't

mean I should give her my baby!"

"*Your* baby?" Rachel covered her mouth, looking horrified.

"No, no, silly," I explained. "She's not mine as in my own flesh and blood. She's mine for another reason."

Now Rachel was totally baffled. I could see it in the way her eyes penetrated mine. "Ya still haven't answered my question," she said. "Where'd this baby come from?"

I was about to tell her everything when Charity started to fuss. I knew she was probably hungry. Only one problem with that, though. I had to figure out a way to get inside the house without running into Mom or Dad. Baby Charity needed a clean bottle and nipple.

"Stay here for a second?" I pleaded.

Rachel nodded, still kneeling.

"If she cries, pick her up," I said. "But whatever you do, stay inside the gazebo. You won't be seen here!" I grabbed the empty baby bottle and ran to the house. Inside, I slipped into the kitchen without making a sound, then ran some hot water at the sink.

Yee-ikes! Dad was up—I could hear him walking around upstairs. My pulse raced as I poured a few drops of dish soap into the bottle, creating lots of suds.

Then I heard footsteps on the steps. Someone was coming! My fingers locked in a frenzy as I poured more water over the bottle, hiding my secret in the sink.

"Morning, hon," Mom said, wearing her bathrobe. Then she did a double take. "Merry? Up so soon?"

Actually, my being up this early wasn't highly unusual. There'd been several days this summer that I'd gotten up to have breakfast with Dad before he left for the hospital. "Morning," I replied, avoiding the question.

She pulled her hair back against her neck and yawned. "It's sweet of you to spend time with your father like this." She headed for the fridge, looking at me for a moment. "Are you washing dishes?"

I was stuck—trapped!

"Uh . . . not really. Just cleaning something I found." It was true.

Worried, I glanced out the window and scanned the gazebo. Good. Everything was still under control. But I realized that if I didn't get some formula into that baby mighty soon, there'd be a major racket going on outside!

"What would you like for breakfast today?" Mom asked, still sounding a bit dazed.

"Scrambled eggs and waffles would be nice," I said, choosing something that would take much longer than cold cereal and toast.

Mom sighed. "Waffles and eggs coming up."

I tried not to be too conspicuous and pushed the bottle down under the soapy water, holding it there. My cat quartet padded across the floor to me. Lily White *meowed* as if to scold me for staying out all night. Shadrach and Meshach did the same. Abednego eyed me with disdain—the powerful silent treatment.

"I'll get your breakfast in a minute," I said. "Just be patient."

Mom closed the refrigerator door and asked, "Are you almost done there, Merry?" She was coming my way!

"Almost." I panicked.

*What could I do now?*

44

# SEVEN

I prayed that something would keep Mom from finding out about the baby bottle. Anything to distract her would be fine.

*Bri-i-ing!* The phone rang and she went to get it.

"Thank you, Lord," I whispered and quickly rinsed the bottle and nipple. Casting a furtive glance in Mom's direction, I dashed out the back door, leaving the cats behind.

Swiftly, I hurried into the gazebo, out of sight. Rachel was doing a good job of keeping Charity quiet—letting her suck on one of her knuckles.

"I hope your hands are clean," I reprimanded her.

"Ya didn't want her hollerin', didja?" Rachel was right. A baby wailing in the backyard was sure to draw unwelcome attention.

I opened the can of formula and poured it into the clean bottle, still warm from washing. A flick of the wrist, and the nipple was in place. "There we are," I said, reaching for Charity.

Rachel backed away, holding Charity close. "Aw, let me feed her."

Resentment gripped me. "But she's . . ."

"She's not yours, any more than I'm yours." Rachel was grinning. "C'mon, just this once?"

I relinquished the bottle and sat down on the floor, close enough to stroke Charity's silky-soft arm. "We've gotta figure out a way to hide her."

"Ach, so now it's *we*?"

"You want to help, right?" I said, noticing how cuddly and contented Charity looked in my friend's arms.

"First, tell me where she came from."

It was only fair to let Rachel in on my secret. Since she was going to be involved, she deserved to know something. "Okay, you win." And I told her enough to satisfy her curiosity.

A bewildered look crossed her face. "Did the truck happen to be noisy?" she asked.

"Yeah. Why?"

Rachel looked down at the baby in her arms. " 'Cause I heard it goin' up and down SummerHill all last week."

"That's weird. Come to think of it, the guy in the truck wanted to know where there was a doctor," I said, remembering.

"How come, do ya think?"

"It's hard to say. Unless . . ."

"What?"

"Unless he's heard that some doctors arrange adoptions for infertile couples."

Rachel's eyes grew sad. "Jah."

"What's wrong?" I asked.

"That would be a terrible heartache, infertility—especially for Amish wives. Most families in our church dis-

46

trict have at least eight children." She sighed. "My second cousin in Ohio could never have babies, though."

"That's too bad," I said. "But your sister-in-law, Sarah, is expecting one this fall, right?"

Rachel brightened. "Jah, come November."

"Won't that be great?" I said. "You'll get to baby-sit your own nephew or niece."

Suddenly, I felt the time pressure, but we talked softly for a few more minutes. I knew I needed to cut this short and go inside to have breakfast with Dad. Otherwise, Mom would suspect something for sure. "Can you hold Charity till I get back?" I asked.

"Where're ya goin' *now*?"

I explained about Mom making eggs and waffles and how I'd sneaked out while she was on the phone. "So will you stay here in the gazebo awhile?"

She shook her head. "I really hafta get back home."

"Rachel! You can't leave yet!"

She stood up, still holding the baby. "I'm sorry, Merry, but I can't stay."

Once again, I felt trapped. "Well, what can I do?" I said, glancing at the house. "Charity can't be left out here alone, and if I don't go in now—"

"I could take Charity with me," Rachel interrupted.

"With you?" I repeated. "That'll never work. How can I keep Charity a secret if you're gonna go show her off at your house?"

"It wouldn't hafta be that way."

"Really? Well, you better talk fast." I listened as she explained.

"I'll keep her wrapped up so no one'll see inside the

basket. She can sleep upstairs in my room for a bit."

Her plan wasn't even remotely close to the way I wanted to handle things, but it seemed to be the only option. "As soon as I can, I'll come over and get her," I said, not knowing what I'd do once I got her home again. "Just please don't tell anyone what I've told you."

Rachel nodded and turned to put Charity in the wicker basket. "I think she needs another change," she said, holding her nose.

"Oh, good idea. *You* do it," I said, digging around in the bottom of the basket for the note. When I found it, Rachel's eyes bugged out.

"What's that?" she asked.

"I'll show you later." I tucked the note into my shorts pocket. "Thanks for helping, Rachel," I said. "You're a lifesaver."

She kept pinching her nose and made a face. Quickly, I left to go to the house.

❧    ❧

"What are *your* plans today?" Dad asked as I spread soft butter on my waffles.

"Oh, I'll probably hang out with Rachel for a while. Maybe clean my room."

Mom sat down for the prayer, and when Dad finished the blessing, she looked up at me suddenly. "Miss Spindler called a little while ago."

"Oh?" My voice squeaked. "Why so early?"

"She wondered what you were doing out in the gazebo with Rachel Zook," Mom said, chuckling. "If she doesn't take the cake!"

"Old Hawk Eyes is up to her old tricks," I said, passing it off in jest. "She lives to spy on people."

Dad glanced at me. The gray hairs around his temple crinkled as he grinned. "Wouldn't it be fun to investigate the old lady—I mean, literally invite ourselves into her house and search it? She must have some high-powered telescope stashed somewhere."

"I think Dad's right." I wanted to pay Old Hawk Eyes a visit in the worst way. What had she seen? I reached for some milk, my throat horribly dry.

"Merry," Mom scolded, "don't wash your food down."

"Sorry," I sputtered, hoping Mom wasn't as curious about my early morning whereabouts as our nosy neighbor.

Dad stirred his herbal tea. "Don't you have a pie or something to take over to Ruby Spindler?" he asked Mom, then winked at me.

"I . . . uh, don't think I have time to probe into Miss Spindler's spying techniques today." I hoped I wasn't reacting too nervously. The last thing I wanted was to stir up suspicion in my parents. A baby's life and future were at stake, and I needed to handle things delicately. I wanted to get Mom and Dad to see their need of another child. And my need of a new sister. Namely, Charity.

Fortunately, the subject of Miss Spindler and her phone call was dropped. Dad kissed Mom's cheek as he excused himself and headed to his study down the hall. Mom hopped up and began clearing the table. "Why don't you run along," she said. "I know you'd probably like to visit with Rachel some more. She might be going to a quilting bee or something. If you don't hurry, you won't catch her."

"Thanks, Mom," I said, giving her a squeeze. She'd played right into my hands. And I was truly grateful!

I ran upstairs and showered and shampooed my hair. It felt good to clean up after having spent the night outside. All the while, I thought of baby Charity. She needed a bath, too, I was certain. And what fun it would be. But where? Where could I take care of her the way I wanted to?

Sweet thoughts of having a baby in the house—in *this* house—made me speed up my morning routine. I brushed my damp hair and pulled it back in a single flat barrette. Opting to skip putting on makeup, I gathered up my dirty T-shirt and shorts. Noticing the full hamper, I smashed them in before I left.

The kitchen was spotless as I breezed through. Mom had already gone upstairs to dress for the day, and Dad was still talking on the phone in his study. I pranced out the back screen door and ran. Already, I missed my baby sister!

I took the shortcut through the willows, praying all the way. If I handled things correctly, Charity could grow up on SummerHill Lane and be my adopted baby sister. God had sent her here—now it was up to me to make the situation work.

Six gray buggies were parked in the side yard at the Zooks'. Concern gripped me as I ran to the back door.

"Merry, *wilkom*!" called Esther Zook through the screen. "Come on in."

I pushed open the door, and Esther came in her long

gray skirt and apron to greet me. But what I saw disturbed me so much I nearly cried. There, in the center of the long, wooden kitchen table, a familiar wicker basket was on display—with Charity the center of attention!

Inwardly, I groaned. What had Rachel done?

My friend caught my eye, appearing rather distraught. She shrugged her shoulders, and I knew something had gone terribly wrong.

I made my way across the enormous kitchen. At least ten Amish women sat around gazing at Charity, talking excitedly in their Pennsylvania Dutch dialect.

"What's going on?" I whispered to Rachel.

She guided me into the dining room. We stood in the corner near a hand-carved cabinet displaying brightly colored china pieces. "Ach, Merry, I would've stopped this from happening if I could've."

"Exactly what happened?"

"Well, it's like this. I took the babe up to my room as ya said to"—her eyes were filled with regret—"but when I left her there to go and help Mam, she started crying. Mam heard Charity hollerin' and came running. The women were already comin' for the quiltin' and, well . . . that's the way it was."

"*Now* what can we do?" I pleaded.

"Don't worry, I didn't tell them she was abandoned," Rachel said. "I knew that would be the wrong thing to say. I said she was visiting you."

I agreed. "Good thinking. But we've got to get her out of here before someone starts asking personal questions."

"Above all, Merry, we mustn't lie," Rachel said, looking even more serious. "T'would not be pleasin' to the Lord."

"You're right. We have to trust God," I said. "He started all this." It felt strange blaming something as precious as a baby's arrival on the Lord. As soon as the words flew out of my mouth, I was sorry.

"I can't go back with ya," Rachel said. "Mam needs me here to help stew chickens for dinner."

"That's fine. Thanks." I gave her a hug. "You did your best, Rachel. Just pray, okay?"

She nodded. "There might be a bit of a problem, though, if Mam finds out about the baby."

"What do you mean?" I felt my heart pound.

"Mam's wantin' another little one. She loves babies, ya see. And she's reached her life change—she can't have more children."

My hopes plunged to the depths. "I knew something like this might happen."

Rachel held my hand. "Don't let envy rob your peace. Remember the Scriptures about coveting. You hafta have a clear head to think, Cousin Merry." She liked to call me *cousin*. We had a common ancestor several generations back that made us bonafide distant relatives.

I sighed, growing more frustrated by the second. Rachel was right about the envy. Only she was forgetting one important piece of information: Charity was not up for grabs. She was mine!

With my heart in my throat, I followed Rachel back into the kitchen. The Amish women were closing in on poor little Charity. One of them reached over and snatched her out of the basket.

Instantly, I remembered the note—the one that had been pinned to Charity's blanket. My head felt dizzy, and I groped for a chair. *Oh no,* I thought. The note was in the pocket of my nylon shorts—in my hamper. And at this moment, Mom was probably sorting the laundry. Discovering my secret!

Tears came to my eyes. I didn't mean to, but I stared at the Amish women talking in a language Charity had never heard. Esther Zook was leaning over their shoulders, touching Charity's face, her hands. What Rachel had said seemed true enough. Her mother would want Charity for her own if she knew the baby girl had been abandoned.

For the third time today, I felt trapped. This time, with absolutely no way out!

# EIGHT

"Ach! What a perty little thing," Rachel's mom was saying. "Whose didja say the baby was?" She was looking at *me* now.

I was tongue-tied. If I told the truth, I might lose Charity. If I lied, I'd lose Rachel's friendship. She was a stickler for honesty.

The whole group of plain women was looking my way, waiting for my answer. I took a deep breath and . . .

Rachel spoke up. "Merry's needin' to get the baby back home now." She went over and took Charity from the plump Amish woman and snuggled her back into the basket.

"I don't think she'll need the blankets today," Esther advised. "The sun's awful hot."

I went over and helped Rachel get Charity settled in. "*Denki* for lettin' me show the baby off," she said to me.

"Thank *you*," I said, and I was sure she knew what I meant by it.

"I'll walk ya to the end of the lane." Rachel held the back kitchen door for me. With a sigh of relief, I escaped down the steps to the sidewalk, carrying Charity.

"Too close for comfort," I muttered.

"You can say that again!" We walked to the end of the sidewalk. Then Rachel touched my arm. "Look who's comin'."

I glanced in the direction of the ramp leading up to the second story of their barn. Levi was heading in our direction. "Merry, s'nice to see ya again," he called.

I glanced at Rachel, wondering what do about Charity. She was already getting fussy being outside in the heat. And what on earth would I tell Levi about her?

"Looks like you've been working hard," I said as Levi approached.

He leaned down and brushed off his jeans. He'd stopped wearing the typical Old Order Amish clothes since his announcement to his family last month about wanting to attend a Bible school. "Well, what do we have here?" He gazed into the wicker basket, obviously interested.

"Uh . . . this is baby Charity," I said, giving Rachel a look that meant *help!*

"Charity?" He smiled that winning smile I'd known all these years. "That's a right good name. Means love, ya know."

I hoped he wouldn't start mentioning his "love" for me in front of his younger sister. Rachel had no idea about the kind of serious talks Levi had initiated weeks ago.

"Well, I better get the baby out of this sun." I turned to go.

Levi, however, didn't let me off the hook so easily. "We need to have a talk sometime 'fore too long," he said, following Rachel and me as we headed for the Zooks' dirt lane.

I knew what he was getting at. He'd be wanting some kind of understanding between us before he left for school, but I wasn't exactly ready to settle down. I wasn't quite fourteen. Even though Amish girls began the courting process at my age, *I* wasn't even close to being ready for such things.

"When can I call on ya, Merry?" he persisted.

"We still have plenty of time." I smiled.

That seemed to satisfy him, and he quit following us and turned and hurried back to the barn.

"Levi's bent on makin' you his wife," Rachel blurted as we headed for the road.

I gasped. "How do you know?"

"I can see it in his eyes," she said. "And the way he talks about ya. He loves ya, Cousin Merry. Honest, he does."

Levi had declared his love last month—in the gazebo, of all places. But I hadn't made any long-term commitment, even though I had to admit I liked him.

"There's a lot of deciding to do, I guess." I looked down at Charity. "But between this little gift from God, and your brother's persistence, things have become mighty chaotic!"

Rachel laughed heartily. "Well then, why don'tcha tell your mother about the baby right away?"

"Because I need time to prepare her—get her thinking about adopting a baby. *Any* baby. Then, when I reveal Charity, she'll be ready. Dad too. It's the only way it'll work," I said, worried that the note from Charity's mother had already been discovered in the hamper.

"Seems to me you've figured it all out," Rachel said.

"Not really," I admitted. "It's just that I know how my parents react to things. If I were to go home with a baby . . . well, first off, Dad would contact the Social Services or the police."

"Police?" She frowned. "What for?"

"To report a missing person or possibly a kidnapping. They would jump to conclusions." In my heart, I hoped baby Charity wasn't either of those.

"Oh, Merry, think of it!" Rachel grabbed my arm, making the basket sway. "What if Charity was kidnapped like you said? What about *that*?"

I hadn't filled her in about the note. Guess now was as good a time as any. "There was a note left with Charity. Pinned to her blanket."

Rachel tugged on her prayer kapp. "You mean to tell me someone deliberately left this baby at your house?"

I shrugged. "Could be. I mean, when you put all the pieces together it kinda fits—the noisy pickup checking out the neighborhood all last week, like you said. And then the way the driver insisted on the girl getting out— telling her she had no choice. Oh, and when he pulled up at my house last evening, he asked if there was a doctor around!"

"You talked to him? Merry, you never said anything about that."

I described everything quickly—how a man in his early twenties had stopped by to ask questions while I was taking pictures of Lissa.

"You're right," she said after hearing it all. "It sounds

like an abandonment. Why don'tcha tell your parents? I don't see why they'd hafta get the police to come."

I sighed, and we kept walking. When we came close to my front yard, I covered Charity with a lightweight blanket, hiding her from view. Just in case. "Run ahead and see if anyone's around back," I told Rachel.

"Jah, just real quick. Then I hafta go back home and help with the quilting."

I waited in the bushes for Rachel to signal.

Seconds passed. What was she doing? Had she encountered someone?

Thoughts of the note being discovered haunted me. I wished Rachel would hurry.

At last, she came—running. Out of breath. "Hurry! All's clear."

"What? You mean it wasn't before?"

"Your mom—she was out hanging up the wash."

"You're kidding? She *never* does that. We have a dryer, for Pete's sake!"

Rachel's eyes grew round as saucers. "Ya don't think she's waitin' for us—suspects somethin', do ya?"

"What are you saying? My mom has no idea about any of this. And I want to keep it that way!" I was completely flustered. Rachel was smack dab in the middle of things, and now I wished I'd overseen all this myself.

"Are ya comin' or not?" she asked.

I shook my head. "We can't risk it. If Mom's hanging out laundry, then she's already found the note."

"Oh, Merry." Her voice was filled with dread.

"There's only one way out," I said, glancing up the hill—way up Strawberry Lane—to Miss Spindler's house.

"Not Old Hawk Eyes," whispered Rachel.

"We have no choice," I replied. "Besides, she already must've seen something going on in the gazebo early this morning. She called my mother to tell her so!"

"*Himmel*," Rachel muttered.

We crouched low and ran across the front yard on the count of three. Baby Charity slept through it, thank goodness. I reminded Rachel of her quilting frolic back home, but she was more interested in the matter at hand. Anyway, we made it around the opposite side of the house without being seen, running from bush to bush, then up . . . up the steep hill behind our house, arriving at last on Miss Spindler's front porch.

We caught our breath for a second, glancing at each other with frightened expressions. "Lord, help us," I pleaded.

"Jah, amen!"

I reached up to pull the heavy gold knocker on the bright red door.

# NINE

Ruby Spindler took her sweet time answering the doorbell. We stood waiting a good thirty seconds before she finally came—whistling.

"My, oh my. Look who's come to call!" She was all made up—lipstick, eyeliner, the works.

"Oh, you're going out," I found myself saying.

"Nonsense!" She opened the door, showing us in as though she'd been expecting us. I wondered about it, but dismissed the thought. Miss Spindler was known all over SummerHill for being a bit eccentric. Today was no exception.

"How's every little thing?" she asked, motioning for us to sit down on her sofa, which was covered with a fresh white sheet. "What brings you dears over to visit this old lady?" She eyed the basket, then Rachel and me.

"It's . . . uh, something very important," I said. "Something top secret."

Rachel nodded but let me do the talking.

"I want to show you something." I leaned over and uncovered Charity.

Miss Spindler was up and out of her chair in a flash.

"Why, in all my born days . . . I never . . ." Her voice trailed off. She reached down and picked Charity right up.

I held my breath, worried that she'd never held an infant before. But I was wrong. Ruby Spindler had a real knack. She cooed at Charity as though she'd been doing it all her life. "Isn't she the most bee-a-u-ti-ful thing you ever did see?" Her eyes were focused on the baby as she spoke.

"Yes, she's beautiful," I agreed, "but . . ." I paused, hoping my words wouldn't sound harsh. "She's been abandoned."

Miss Spindler's gaze shot up to meet mine. "Abandoned, you say? How could anyone in their right mind do such a thing? Why, she's gorgeous. Simply gorgeous."

I secretly congratulated myself on this surprising turn of events. Miss Spindler was actually very good with Charity, whose little eyes were starting to open as the old lady rocked her and talked in a sing-song way.

"Miss Spindler, I . . . uh . . . *we*," I looked at Rachel, suddenly feeling it was wise to include her in this. "Rachel and I wondered if you might be able to keep Charity for a little while."

Her head jerked up. "Keep her? Here?"

"Just for a short time," I said. "While I talk to my parents about some things." I went on, careful not to explain too much about my plan to convince my parents.

"Heavens to Betsy, you don't have to hem and haw about something like this, Merry Hanson. Just out with it! You need someplace to hide this here little one, ain't so?"

"Hide?"

She smiled a peculiar, almost uncanny, smile. "Ah yes, I saw you last evening. And again this morning. Hiding in the gazebo, you were." She cackled a bit.

I shot a concerned look at Rachel. "You didn't tell anyone, did you?"

Miss Spindler waved her bony hand. "Never you mind 'bout that."

I had to know. "But you didn't tell my mother when you called—about the baby, did you?"

"Not on your life," she replied. "I saw what happened. That there feller in the pickup—my lands, what a sad state of affairs!"

I stood up. "You saw? But how?" Our house blocked her view—it was virtually impossible for her to have seen him. I was sure of it.

She shook her head. "There, there. Don't go worryin' yourself over such trivia. The fact remains, the babe's been left behind. Now you two run along. I'll take good care of my little dumplin' here." And she rocked away, calling the baby her precious angel over and over.

I went to say goodbye to Charity—the gift God had most obviously sent to *me*. She gripped my finger in her tiny fist. But her blue eyes were fixed on Miss Spindler.

I was torn between relief and worry. Now I was free to work on my original plan with Mom and Dad, but what about Miss Spindler? What if she got wrapped up in Charity while I set things in motion with my family?

"You don't mind, do you?" I asked, almost wishing she'd hand the baby back to me.

"Scoot!" she said, shooing us out the door. "Just let

me know when you want her back. In the meantime, I'll bathe her and buy her some new clothes."

*Bathe her?* Old Hawk Eyes was going to give my future sister a bath? Buy her clothes? Spoil her the way I'd wanted to? I could see this was already way out of control.

Rachel and I scarcely spoke as we headed down Strawberry Lane to the corner and turned left toward my house.

"I guess you have a quilting to attend," I said softly.

"Jah, I do."

We hugged, and tears came to my eyes as she left. For the first time since I'd carried the baby basket into Miss Spindler's house, my arm ached. And now, so did my heart.

☙   ❧

It was next to impossible getting Mom's and Dad's attention later at supper. Mom kept talking about how lovely it had been today. "Not hot and muggy—just nice," she said. "I even decided to hang the laundry out for a change. Oh, and it smelled so fresh when I brought it in."

I was afraid she was secretly trying to tell me about the note she'd found in my shorts, but nothing came of it. I even fished around, asking leading questions, but she didn't volunteer a thing.

Soon, something else was on her mind—the church potluck a week from tomorrow. And Dad? He began recounting several hectic experiences from his day at the hospital.

More than anything, I was dying to know if Mom had

found the note in my shorts. I'd checked the hamper first thing when I returned from Miss Spindler's, but the clothes had already gone through Mom's super-systematized sorting process. In fact, all my dirty shorts from the entire week were flapping in the breeze when I hurried outside later. Unfortunately, the pockets of the gray nylon shorts were one-hundred-percent-amen empty.

Since the table conversation seemed to be going in several different directions, I decided to postpone my discussion about the baby until dessert. From past experience, I knew it would be futile to work up to something this controversial. And I certainly didn't want my parents to become suspicious at that type of approach, so I barreled full steam ahead. Skip, my brother, had paved the way with this sort of tactic. Being younger, I'd learned more from him than I cared to admit.

Mom set a piece of black raspberry pie in front of each of us. Dad reached for his fork and took the first bite while Mom and I watched. It was a kind of game. Mom waited eagerly for his response, and Dad, being the ham he was, dragged out the suspense, rolling his eyes, licking his lips. Finally, he said, "It's absolutely delicious."

Mom grinned and picked up her fork. *Now* it was time for the baby discussion. . . .

"I think we need another kid around here," I announced. "A baby, maybe?"

I could hear the grandfather clock ticking in the hallway. I took a breath and kept going. "I mean, don't you think we ought to have another sister for me? Not to replace Faithie or anything, but it would be nice."

Dad looked straight at Mom. "What did you put in

Merry's pie? I certainly didn't get any of it."

I sat up. "Dad! I'm serious."

His jawline was firm. "That's what I'm talking about. You had something very strange to eat. Or was it the iced tea?" He looked around, inspecting Mom's tea glass, then reaching for mine.

"It's not a joke!" I insisted.

"Merry, please," Mom said. "You seem all worked up about this. Does this have anything to do with Faithie's . . . anniversary?"

I got up from the table, tears coming fast. "I just wish people would take me seriously once in a while."

Dad reached out as I ran past him and into the hallway. "Merry?" he called. "I didn't mean to . . ."

I couldn't hear the rest of what he said. But I knew he'd had fun at my expense. And it hurt.

Upstairs, I found refuge in my room. The cats followed me to my bed, where I collapsed, feeling sorry for myself. "You guys never have any problems, do you?" I said as they came to comfort me with their sweet, furry heads and whiskers. "You sleep, eat, and sleep again. Must be nice."

Abednego didn't appreciate what I'd said. He whined his best retaliatory *meow*. Twice.

I pouted, staring at the wall on the opposite side of the room. The wall where my best photography had been framed and hung. My wall gallery, I'd always called it.

Sadly, I tried to imagine a picture of Charity up there—holding my finger with her viselike grip as I held her in my arms. I'd have to set up my tripod for a shot like that.

The thought was enticing, but I knew a photo of the abandoned baby would only end up haunting me. *If only my parents were more understanding,* I thought, blaming the negative events of the day on them. I turned on the radio and listened for a while—until Dad knocked on my door.

"Honeybunch," he said, using the nickname he used when I was in trouble or upset. "Mind if I come in?"

I minded, but I wasn't rude. I sat up and held Abed-nego next to my face—a defense against whatever Dad was going to say. "The door's open," I called, still wishing . . . hoping things might turn out in my favor.

# TEN

Dad sat at the end of the bed. "I'm sorry about teasing you," he began. "It was uncalled for."

His subdued expression gave me courage, and I nodded. "Maybe you and Mom didn't understand what I was saying earlier." I wanted to give him the benefit of the doubt.

"Having a baby would be terribly rough on your mother at her age," he explained.

I shook my head. "That's *not* what I meant. You jumped to conclusions."

"Then I'm totally in the dark here. Why don't you tell me what's on your mind, Mer?"

I thought about Charity—hidden away at Miss Spindler's—and how she belonged here. "What if we *adopted* a baby?"

Mom was standing in the doorway now. I knew by her dubious look that she'd heard what I said. "Don't you think your father and I ought to be the ones deciding something like that?"

"I know," I replied. "It's something that has to be thought through. People just don't jump into embracing someone else's child as their own." I'd read that some-where—it sounded good. Besides, I needed to make some points with my parents, who by now looked too shocked for words.

"Merry, is something bothering you?" Dad asked, frowning. "Do we need to talk about Faithie?"

"This is about *me*, not Faithie," I said, but deep in-side, I knew the arrival of baby Charity was linked to Faithie—at least in my mind. Desperately, I wanted to share with them the dream I'd had last night in the ga-zebo. To make them see the truth about little Charity. That she was God's gift—my second chance for a sister.

Dad patted the bed beside him, and Mom sat down. The two of them, along with my four cats, studied me. I tried various approaches in my head, but none of them worked. Honestly, I couldn't think of anything to say without giving away my secret.

At last, Dad spoke. "Would it help if we didn't visit Faithie's graveside this year?"

I couldn't believe he'd said that! "I told you this has nothing to do with Faithie. It's something I really want—for us to adopt a baby. Couldn't you and Mom at least *think* about it?"

It was my best shot.

Dad looked at Mom and reached for her hand. "As far as I'm concerned, this isn't the best time for either of us to be starting over," he stated. "Babies take an incred-ible amount of time and energy."

Mom interjected, "Your father's nearly fifty, and we're both very busy with our present responsibilities." Her voice grew softer. "Someday, *you'll* have babies,

Merry. When you're finished with college and have a husband."

My logical approach was getting me nowhere fast. The tone of Mom's voice told me she needed an emotional push. Something to jump-start her maternal instincts.

"Okay, let's just say, for the sake of discussion, that an abandoned baby is found somewhere around SummerHill. And what if that baby is a beautiful baby girl with no one to love her and provide for her?"

Mom's eyes were transfixed, and Dad was listening intently. I had them!

I continued. "What if the baby is so precious and adorable that the person who found her wants to keep her? And what if the person knows for sure that the baby is meant to be in that person's life?"

Dad scratched his chin, trying to hide his stunned expression. "My goodness, what a hypothetical situation you've cooked up."

Mom didn't wait for me to answer. She stood up and walked over to the window. "What would *I* do if I found an abandoned baby?" she asked, redirecting the question. "Well, that's rather simple, I would think. Right, hon?" She glanced at Dad.

He nodded. "First thing—we'd have to report a missing child. After all, the police should be notified in order to locate the mother."

Dad had thrown a wrench into my setup. And worse, Mom was following his line of reasoning.

"Well, what if the person who found the baby knew

Gerhardt

the baby had been purposely abandoned?" I said. "What then?"

Dad mentioned the possibility of kidnapping, completely ignoring my comment. "Unfortunately, babies are taken out from under their parents' noses every year in this country. Some are sold into the black market. Others are left to die or simply abandoned on someone's doorstep. How would the person who'd found such a baby know the child hadn't been kidnapped?" He leaned back on the bed, his hands supporting his head.

I sighed. Why were they making this so difficult? "To begin with, I just said 'what if' the person knew somehow that the baby was *not* kidnapped, but abandoned."

Dad's eyes closed as he spoke. "Merry, why don't you just level with us? Do you know someone who has found such a baby?"

I was frantic! He'd seen through it. I should've known Dad would read between the lines. Mom too.

"Guess neither of you were born yesterday." I started to explain. "Yes, a baby has been found. She's an adorable baby girl . . . and she's ours—God showed me that." I left out the part about the dream.

I told them the truth. "I was the one who found her—in a wicker laundry basket last night—in the gazebo."

Mom turned and stared. Dad was sitting upright now, the lines in his forehead creased into a deep frown. "Someone left a baby in our gazebo?"

"Merry, why didn't you tell us?" Mom asked.

"It's a long story," I whispered. But I proceeded to tell them everything, even about the note in my shorts.

Mom gasped. "There was a note, too?"

"I put it in my gray shorts, and then forgot and tossed them in the laundry," I explained. "Silly me."

Mom put both hands on top of her head. "Oh, dear. I found several things in your pockets, but I don't think I threw them away. I believe they're still on the counter in the—"

Before she finished, I left the room to find the note. It was exactly the proof I needed. As I rushed through the kitchen toward the cellar steps, I stopped to look out the window. The lights in Miss Spindler's house were beginning to come on. It was dusk, close to the hour when baby Charity had come to me yesterday. I stared at the tall two-story house an acre away. How I missed my sweet little Charity!

Quickly, I turned and ran downstairs to retrieve the note.

&#8477; &#8477;

By the end of the evening—after pleading with Dad not to call the police (he did anyway) and giving a complete description of the old pickup and the people in it—I knew there was only the faintest hope for Charity's future with us. But I hung on to the hope tenaciously, prayerfully. When it came right down to it, the baby's future rested with the police's ability to track down a clanking, blue pickup with an abusive driver and a tearful young woman. The rest was up to God.

Which brings me to Miss Spindler and the disturbing evening visit with the baby of my dreams.

# ELEVEN

Miss Spindler seemed quite distracted when I showed up on her doorstep. "Come in," she said, treating me more like a stranger than the close neighbor I was.

"Where's Charity?" I asked, looking around.

"Ah, you came to see my baby."

The preoccupied expression on her wrinkled face had me downright worried. "I've come to get Charity. My father has just talked to the police."

"Police?"

I nodded. It seemed as hard for her to accept as it had been for me. "It's procedure," I explained. "They'll take her to Social Services until they can determine where her parents are." The lump in my throat made it hard to talk. "If she's declared an orphan or abandoned, Dad'll talk to his administrative friends on the Social Services board about putting her in temporary foster care—with us, if all goes well." *And if I can talk my parents into it,* I thought.

"My, oh, my," she muttered, fluttering around in a daze. "Going and reporting Charity missing? Why, the little darlin's been right here all the time."

She was crazy-out-of-her-mind distressed. "Miss

Spindler . . . I'm so sorry. I never should've—"

"Nonsense! That youngster has been just what the doctor ordered. A godsend . . . yes indeedy," she said. "This lonely old woman has missed so much in life, and now . . ." Her words floated away.

She'd mentioned God, and I felt upset. How could she latch on to Charity as though the Lord had sent the baby to *her*? Careful not to let her see my irritation, I nodded, trying to think of something soothing to say. "If we pray," I said, "and if it's God's will—which I believe it is— then Charity will be right back here."

Miss Spindler's blue-gray hair was curled up in bobby pins all over her head, and she wore an ankle-length white duster. She sat down in an overstuffed chair, and for a moment I thought she was going to cry. Her voice wavered as she told about going to town to buy an infant car seat, disposable diapers, and blankets. "Aw, you should see her dressed up in her new things. She looks right fine—like an angel, if I must say so myself."

"You spent money on the baby?" I was truly amazed at her confession.

"Spent the entire afternoon rounding up all sorts of baby things," she said proudly. "I even stopped to see one of my dear old friends at the nursing home and showed Charity off." She grinned, showing her gums. "And don'tcha know—I loved every single second of it!"

*Poor Old Hawk Eyes. She's gotten too attached.*

"Whatcha lookin' at, dear?" she asked.

Sadness for the little lady nearly got the best of me as I stood there in her old-fashioned parlor. Quickly, I looked away so as not to embarrass her. "So," I said in almost a whisper, "that's where we stand with Charity."

Without another word, Miss Spindler pulled herself up out of the easy chair and went upstairs. I thought of Dad's comment earlier this morning about someone coming into Miss Spindler's house and searching it for spy equipment. The thought helped to lighten my tension.

Miss Spindler was gone only a few minutes before bringing Charity down.

Half asleep, the baby opened her eyes. *Blue as blue can be,* I thought.

"Hello, again," I said, reaching out for her little fist. "I missed you so much, but I know Auntie Ruby here took extra-good care of you."

Miss Spindler was nodding and beaming. "That, she did."

It nearly broke my heart to remove Charity from the old woman's arms. She helped me wrap Charity in several blankets before we headed out. Then she went about filling the wicker basket full of cans of formula, diapers, and other baby things.

"There's a dear," she whispered as I stepped onto her front porch weighed down with everything. "Goodbye, Angel." She touched the baby's head lightly. "God be with you."

I wanted to reach out and hug Old Hawk Eyes. She'd surprised me with her kind, nurturing ways, and I was grateful. "Thanks for your help," I said before walking out into the night sweetly fragranced with honeysuckle.

"I'll leave the yard light on for you, dear." Miss Spindler stood on the porch and watched as I headed down the hill toward my house.

"Thanks again!" I called, knowing full well the people from Social Services would be showing up any minute.

Arriving home, I hurried into the house. Mom was waiting at the kitchen door for me. For *Charity* and me.

In a few seconds, Mom was talking baby talk and making over Charity as if she'd never laid eyes on such a pretty baby.

"Will you look at those blue eyes," Mom said as Dad came into the room.

"Now, remember what I said," he admonished. "Don't fall head over heels for a baby that most likely won't be . . ."

Mom held the baby out to him. Reluctantly, he took Charity and held her up to his face. "Lookee here," he said, sounding something like Miss Spindler's crotchety old voice. "Well, what do we have here?"

"So what do you say?" I said, pushing for an instant decision. "Can we adopt her?"

Mom and Dad were shoulder to shoulder, peering into the face of baby Charity—my gift from God. I tried to make conversation several more times to no avail. It was amazing—a transformation was taking place before my eyes. For people who'd just said they were much too old and had way too many responsibilities to add to their family at this late date, well . . . the way things looked from my perspective, the Social Services people could wait and show up tomorrow or the next day. Or never.

Suddenly, Dad pushed Charity into my arms. "Here, hold her for a minute." He dashed off to his study, and I heard him close the door. My heart was in my throat.

"What's Dad doing?" I asked.

Mom leaned her head close to Charity's. "Oh, you might just be surprised."

"What?" I pleaded. "Is he calling someone important?"

"Your father, as you know, is easily swayed when it comes to people with terminal illnesses, emergency situations, and . . . *babies*," she reminded me.

"I was counting on that." I grinned down at Charity. This time she was gazing up at me. "Oh, you're so pwecious."

Abednego and his brothers wandered into the kitchen just then. Abednego gave me the evil eye as if to say: *Put that human baby down this instant!*

I scolded him. "You get plenty of love and attention. Now, go find your adopted sister!" And I shooed them outside to look for Lily White.

Mom pulled out a kitchen chair for me. "I'd better give Miss Spindler a quick call," she said. "It would be nice to know when Charity had her last bottle."

Her words were music to my ears. And as I waited for her to chat with our nosy neighbor, I prayed that the person Dad was talking to on the phone would bend the rules and let us keep Charity until she was free to be adopted. "And if not, Lord," I whispered, "at least let us keep her tonight."

It was a long shot, but from what I knew of my heavenly Father, the God of the universe took great delight in performing miraculous feats.

# TWELVE

The phone rang just as Dad was coming out of his study. He hurried back to answer it. I waited for him to return, hugging Charity close. Then he called to me. "The phone's for you, Merry."

I picked up the kitchen phone, holding Charity in one arm. "Hello?" I said, looking down at the darling baby.

"Hi, Merry." It was Lissa Vyner. "Just wondered if you got the film developed that you took of me yesterday."

I'd completely spaced it out. "Not yet. But I'll get Mom to take it down to the one-hour place tomorrow," I promised. "It's just that so much has been happening since you were here. You'll never believe what . . ."

Dad was waving at me, signaling to me.

"Uh . . . just a minute, Lissa." I handed Charity to Mom.

Dad hurried over and covered the phone with his hand. "Don't mention anything about the baby just yet," he advised. "Lissa doesn't know it, but her dad just did me a big favor at the police department."

I knew Officer Vyner was on the Lancaster police

force. He and Dad had become acquaintances because of Lissa's and her mother's attendance at our church. More recently, Dad had teamed up with Lissa and me to persuade him to come to the church potluck next weekend.

"Okay, I won't say anything," I said as he handed the phone back to me. I hesitated when I got on the phone again. "So, Lissa, how's everything?"

"Merry? You were starting to tell me something," she urged, not letting me change the subject. "You were saying something about all that's been happening. Did that weird guy in the pickup show up again?"

"That's not exactly what I was talking about." I was hedging, not knowing what to say next.

Dad must've sensed my distress. "Tell her you'll call back," he whispered, moving his hand in a circular motion in midair.

"My dad's waiting to talk to me. Can I call you later?"

"Sure. But—"

"Okay then," I said and hung up.

Dad and Mom looked like Siamese twins as they stood together in the kitchen hovering over Charity, who was obviously soaking up their attention.

"What did Lissa's dad say about the baby?" I asked. I had to walk over and stand in front of them, waving my arms. "Yoo-hoo! Remember me?"

At last, Dad tore his gaze away from Charity's face. "Oh, I'm sorry, Merry. What is it?"

I asked him again about the arrangement. "Did Officer Vyner say we could keep Charity overnight?"

He nodded. "We've got her for the night"—and here he turned and kissed Mom—"possibly several days."

"Really?" I squealed with delight. "That long?"

"Until the in-state tracking is done," he said. "By the way, Merry, hang on to that note from the mother. A handwriting analyst may be called in on the case."

My heart sank. "I don't want to help them find Charity's mother," I wailed. "She doesn't deserve our baby!"

Dad's eyes clouded a bit. "According to the law, she must be punished for this act of desertion."

"But what if they don't find her or the guy she was with?"

"One step at a time," Dad said gently, glancing at Mom, who looked smitten with baby love. "Try to be patient. Remember what the proverb says: 'Be patient and you will finally win. . . . ' "

I backed away from the three of them and glanced out the window at Miss Spindler's house. "Someone *else* is anxious for Charity to stay around here, too."

Mom heard me. "Miss Spindler, right?"

"And she's not the only one." I told them about the Amish women next door, particularly Esther Zook.

"Well, we don't have to worry about the Amish community causing us trouble," Dad said. "They don't get caught up in legal hassles."

"Must be nice," I said, contemplating the time involved in locating an abandoned baby's parents, especially if they didn't want to be found. I turned toward Mom and the baby in her arms. "It seems like everyone around here wants to claim her."

There was no arguing that point. Even Dad nodded his head in agreement. "She's a dumpling," he said. "But we have to do the right thing by her, whether she stays with us or not." Dad usually didn't speak out strongly about his beliefs, so it surprised me to hear him talk this way. But one thing was certain, he wanted Charity as much as I did. So did Mom!

My first hurdle was history. Now if I could just get past the next few days of waiting. Would the police be able to catch up with the rattletrap pickup and its occupants? And what about Miss Spindler? Had she lost her heart to Charity, too? I felt sorry for her—and for putting her in the middle of this.

# THIRTEEN

I felt even worse Saturday morning when Miss Spindler came over with a handful of crocheted baby booties. I met her at the back door, noting that she'd done her hair up in its usual gray-blue puff. Her cheeks had a splash of color in them, and I couldn't tell if it was rouge or if she was simply excited to see the baby again.

"Hello, dear," she said. "I stayed up late making these booties for Charity."

I looked at them—four or five adorable pairs of pink, pink-and-white, and variegated colors. "These are darling!"

"Why, thank you, Merry." She looked around, and I knew I had to invite her in. "Is the little sweetie up?"

"Come with me." I led her upstairs to the guest room across from my parents' bedroom. "We fixed up a room for her—at least for now."

Mom was powdering the baby on a makeshift changing table, actually an antique cherry dresser. She'd made it comfortable for Charity with some waterproof pads and a soft, thick towel.

"Aw, there's a love," Miss Spindler sputtered as we stood in the doorway.

"Look what Miss Spindler made." I showed Mom the booties.

"Why, Ruby," Mom said, turning toward Old Hawk Eyes, "what a thoughtful thing."

Miss Spindler bent over and kissed Charity's head. "How's every little thing with our dapple dumplin' today?" Charity kicked her feet and tried to grab Miss Spindler's long nose.

"I think she recognizes her auntie Ruby," I said, hoping to ease the awkward situation. It was clear how much the old lady adored the baby.

Mom snapped the baby outfit and held Charity up, goo-gooing close to her face. "She's really a very placid baby," Mom mentioned. "Hardly fussed all night."

"Well, I declare," Miss Spindler said. "She fits right in here, doesn't she?"

Mom handed the baby to our neighbor. "Here, she likes you, too, Ruby." That brought a broad smile to the wrinkled face.

I let the two of them chitchat alone. Quietly, I slipped out of the room and down the long upstairs hall to my room, where I got my camera. I was careful to remove the old film—the film of Lissa posing in her bridesmaid dress—and load it with fresh film. That's when I remembered my promise to call Lissa back. Because of all the excitement, I'd forgotten. Well, not really forgotten—just couldn't pull myself away from Charity and the remarkable way my parents were responding to her.

Last night, Dad had gone to the attic and lugged

down two matching pine cradles—one was mine, the other Faithie's. "We'll need one upstairs and one down," he'd explained as Mom watched incredulously from the attic steps.

"While you're up there," I'd said, "could you bring down some of my old baby dresses? Charity needs a dress to wear on Sunday."

Dad was more than willing to pile up a bunch of my baby clothes and carry them down. In fact, he was so taken with Charity, he was nearly late for work this morning. And for a summer Saturday, I was up earlier than usual, too. There was only one reason, of course.

While Mom and Miss Spindler talked and cooed at the baby, I took unposed shots of the three of them and several close-ups of Charity. Miss Spindler made me promise to give her some reprints when I got them developed.

"I'd be happy to," I told her. And it was true. With my parents in the picture, Miss Spindler no longer seemed like a threat.

Later, while Mom and I were fixing lunch, I experienced a twinge of sadness for my brother, Skip, away at camp. He was missing out on the new addition to the Hanson household.

"What do you think Skip would say about having Charity here?" I asked Mom.

"Oh, you know Skip. He takes things in stride."

Mom was probably right. After all, he'd survived his breakup with Nikki Klein, Jonathan's older sister, a few weeks ago. I didn't feel too badly about it, though, probably because I didn't think Nikki and Skip were right for each other. Besides, Skip had decided on a future in medicine, and he had years of schooling ahead of him.

"Do you think Skip'll miss us when he goes off to college?" I probed.

Mom sighed, as though she wasn't ready to think about losing her only son just yet. "Well, Skip has always been a very independent person, as you know."

*Obnoxious too,* I thought.

Mom continued. "I think he will do just fine. Now, why don't you run and check on Charity before we sit down for lunch?" I knew it was my cue to back off about Skip. Mom was super-sensitive about her kids. It had only been the day before yesterday that she and I had been able to talk openly about Faithie's death. After seven years!

I took her lead and kept quiet. Tiptoeing into the dining room, I peeked at our baby. She was snoozing peacefully in Faithie's cradle, a heavy pine piece with a honey stain that looked antique—exactly the way Mom had requested it be made. Since antiques were one of her ongoing obsessions, the cradle was ideal.

I touched it, rocking it gently as I looked into her sweet face. "Please don't ever leave us," I whispered. "I couldn't bear to lose you."

Hesitantly, I thought about tomorrow—July thirty-first—the anniversary I'd been somewhat dreading. Would we take Charity to visit Faithie's graveside? How would my twin sister *really* feel if she knew about Charity?

"Merry?" Mom was calling.

I hurried back into the kitchen, my mind beginning to fill with troubling thoughts. My worry escalated even more when Dad called midafternoon. Mom's face turned ashen as she held the phone, listening.

"What is it?" I whispered.

Her eyes grew wide, and she shushed me. "Where?" she was saying. "In Maryland?"

I put my hand on my heart, hoping this wasn't about finding Charity's parents.

Finally, Mom got off the phone. She hurried into the dining room, staring down at Charity in the cradle. "Oh, Merry," she whispered, hugging me. "The police have located the blue pickup."

"Oh, please . . . no." I could say no more. My hands gripped into a fist, and I wanted to fly away with Charity. Far, far away, where no one could take her from us!

## FOURTEEN

I felt mighty droopy as I sat out front on the porch waiting for Dad. Mom had taken Charity into town for her required visit to Social Services. Since Dad had arranged temporary foster care with us, I wasn't worried about losing her to the system. It was that horrible APB and the police investigation that made me frantic.

Evidently, the blue pickup had been deserted somewhere near Baltimore, Maryland. Mom had filled me in on everything Dad told her on the phone. The driver and young woman had left no trace as to their whereabouts, but they were definitely being hunted. The pickup had been registered, but not insured. I shuddered to think of Charity having to grow up with irresponsible parents.

I remembered last night. Troubled, I had stayed up late praying, then insisted on holding Charity till she fell asleep. Mom seemed to understand my need to be near her. She and Dad were showing signs of the same. When I'd finally relinquished Charity to the guest room across the hall from them, I noticed Miss Spindler's light was on, too. I wondered if she was thinking about Charity and the new things she'd bought her. My foster sister needed much more than clothes at the moment. She needed a miracle—we all did!

Now, as I sat on the front porch stroking my cats and waiting for Dad, I talked out loud to God. "Please take care of this situation, Lord. You know how much we love Charity . . . how much we want her to stay with us."

Soon, I heard a car coming down SummerHill. I leaned forward, straining to see if it was Dad. It wasn't. I sighed, leaning back, wishing he'd hurry. But the car pulled into the driveway. Out hopped Levi Zook!

"Hi," I said, getting up and going to meet him. "Is this your new car?"

"Jah," he said. "Do ya like it?"

"It's great." I stepped back and surveyed the shimmering white Mustang, washed and waxed—very classy. "Where do you hide it?"

"I don't hafta anymore," he said. "But don't worry, I wouldn't think of flauntin' it in my father's face."

"Oh," I said, thinking about another father out there somewhere in Maryland or beyond. Charity's father.

"Merry, are ya all right?" Levi looked concerned.

I wasn't prepared for an in-depth explanation of the past two days of my life. Not now.

"It's Faithie's home-going anniversary tomorrow, jah?"

I nodded. "But I'm okay with it."

He reached for my hand. "I'd be happy to go along if it's okay with your family."

"To the cemetery?" This was a first. How serious *was* Levi about me? When I found my voice again, I said, "Skip's off at camp, so maybe you could take his place."

He nodded, fooling with his suspenders. "There's somethin' I hafta tell ya, Merry. I'm gonna be leavin' sooner than I planned." His voice was firm, resolute. "Before I go, there are some things we hafta discuss."

"When are you leaving?"

"In two weeks. August thirteenth."

"You're right," I said. "We *do* need to talk." I'd been putting this off long enough. Unfortunately, I'd been so involved with Charity and her future, I'd ignored my own.

"Can ya go for a ride with me?" he asked.

"Not now. Dad'll be home any minute."

"Will ya ask if I can take ya for a hamburger when he comes?" Levi looked so boyish and cute. I hated to think of him going off to Bible school, leaving SummerHill behind.

"I'll ask, but I probably shouldn't tonight." I didn't want to miss out on any new developments with Charity's birth parents. It would be truly horrible to go off and have a good time with Levi only to come home and find Charity was gone.

"I could give ya a call later," he said. "I'll be down at the Yoders' place for a bit. They have a phone in their woodshop, ya know."

"Okay." I could see Levi was getting a kick out of saying he'd call me. The Old Order Amish didn't believe in having telephones in the houses they owned. Levi had grown up without one all these years. His connections with Mennonite friends had pulled him away from the old Amish ways of his youth. He was a changed person now—not entirely in dress, although his hair looked like Skip's or any other modern boy's around. And he was determined to win the world for Christ—another strong Mennonite influence—one that Jesus himself taught His disciples. It was the command Levi was hanging his hat on. And his future as a minister.

"I'll call ya after supper, then," he said, his eyes shining with hope.

"I really like your car." I wasn't kidding. It was really cool. The Levi of the past obviously had incorporated his passion for wheels into this modern-day form of transportation. I knew even as I stood there waving that if Charity weren't in the middle of my life, I'd be saying absolutely yes to a drive with Levi.

I watched him drive his shiny car down SummerHill and park it quite a ways past his father's farm. What a guy! He'd had the gumption to make the break from the Amish for his own beliefs' sake, and the sake of spreading the Gospel. Yet he was careful to show respect to his parents by not flaunting—as he said—his modern wheels and his decision to go to Bible school. I admired him with renewed interest. I could hardly wait for our talk.

Dad showed up soon after Levi left, and I ran out to the driveway to meet him.

"When will we know if Charity can be ours?" was the first thing out of my mouth.

"Well," he chuckled, "it's nice to see you, too."

I apologized. "But I'm dying to find out something. How long do we have to wait before Charity's free to adopt?"

"Patience, Merry," he chided gently.

"It's too hard to be patient sometimes," I admitted.

"Why not enjoy Charity while we have her?"

"But what if she has to go back . . . to her family?" The thought nearly killed me.

"We'll deal with that when and if the time comes," he stated, and I knew he hoped it would never happen. We walked into the house together. "Your mother should be home any minute now. What do you say we surprise her and make supper?" It was a great idea. Only one problem: Dad didn't know the first thing about cooking.

"Guess we're talking pizza, right?" I teased.

He grinned. "You make the salad. I'll preheat the oven."

"Count on it." I went to the fridge and pulled out some salad fixings. Dad was in an interesting mood. One I hadn't seen in ages. I hoped his sparkling, fun-loving attitude would last, but I honestly wondered how he'd feel tomorrow. Tomorrow afternoon—when we visited Faithie's grave.

# FIFTEEN

I rushed to the back door when I heard Mom coming. Eagerly, I scooped up Charity from Mom's arms and hurried back into the kitchen. Dad and I had set the table, complete with candles. The mood was festive—after all, we had a lot to be festive about.

"Charity needs to be in on our celebration," I said.

"What celebration?" Mom asked.

"The let's-enjoy-having-Charity-around-for-no-matter-how-long celebration," I replied.

Mom looked puzzled at first. Then she glanced at Dad, whose contented expression must've helped her understand.

"Bring the little munchkin to me," Dad said, holding out his arms. While he held her, I scrambled into the dining room to get the cradle. It was heavy—well constructed, too. Handmade by one of the Yoder boys' Amish uncles before Faithie and I were born.

I carried it into the kitchen, setting it down in the middle of the room. "There," I said, "now we can all see Charity while we eat."

Mom went to wash her hands at the sink. "I'm afraid

the little stinker won't make it much longer. We'd better get started."

"You mean she's hungry?" I asked.

Mom dried her hands. "She certainly didn't seem interested in eating while we waited our turn at Social Services. I ended up putting a blanket down on the floor and letting her kick her feet. She cooed and gurgled at everyone. Quite a social butterfly."

I could visualize the scene. "I'll bet you had tons of visitors swooning over her, right?"

Mom nodded. "You should've seen the people coming up and asking about her—how old she was, what was her name. Standard baby questions." Mom smiled and went over to take Charity from Dad. "But, you know, I felt wonderful. Really wonderful." Her eyes were moist as she looked at Dad. "Better than I have in years."

I wondered exactly what Mom was thinking. The tender glances exchanged between my parents were apparently not meant to include me. But even though I was the outsider for the moment, something in me rejoiced as I stood in our familiar old country kitchen, in our ancient colonial house—the place my twin sister and I had come home to—watching the lines in my mother's face soften. Had Charity's coming soothed her pain, too?

❧   ❧

Once Charity was settled in her cradle perch, Dad prayed and we ate supper. He recounted the emergency-room events of his day for Mom and me. Soon, Mom was going over every inch of her day spent with Charity and me, telling about Miss Spindler's visit—and all the handmade booties—as well as every baby-related happening in the last nearly ten hours Dad had been gone.

I grinned, listening, and wondered how it had been in this grand old house when Faithie and I were babies. Before I could even bring it up, Mom started talking about the days of double everything.

"Goodness, I don't know how I kept up with things." She reached over and let her hand rest on top of mine. "Merry was the happiest baby. She could entertain herself for hours at a time." Mom smiled, reliving the days.

"That's why you named me Merry, right?"

"You never cried when you were born," she explained. "At least, it didn't sound like crying."

Dad agreed. "You laughed . . . cackled, I guess you'd say."

"Cackled?" This was the first I'd heard my birth described *that* way.

Dad rubbed his chin. "You're not going to argue with me, are you? After all, I was there—I know what I heard." Dad was laughing now, and Mom, too. Charity started to join in, at least that's how it sounded at first, but her fussy cooings gave way to hearty cries.

"Uh-oh," Mom said, turning around. "Another country heard from." She warmed up the baby's formula while Dad and I argued over who would get to feed her. Dad won out, but only because I let him. I knew it wouldn't be long before he'd be sound asleep in his easy chair. Then, it would be my turn!

"I can't wait till Charity's finally ours," I said, watching Dad hold the baby with bottle tilted up.

Mom didn't say anything, but in a few seconds, Dad

did. Again, his words were measured and directed toward Mom. "Have you decided what you want to do if Charity becomes available for adoption?"

A wistful look played around Mom's lips. "Well, hon, I've been praying about it, but I think we should talk—"

The phone rang.

"I'll get it," I said, jumping up. "Hello?"

"Hullo, Merry. This is Levi."

I laughed, stretching the phone cord around the corner into the dining room. "I know who you are."

"Well, didja have a chance to ask?"

*Ask?* Once again, I'd forgotten. Charity was taking over my entire life!

"Merry, I wanna see ya." His voice was mellow and sweet.

"Uh . . . just a minute." I covered up the phone and went back into the kitchen. However, I had to wait to ask until Dad quit kissing Mom—on the lips. "Excuse me," I said when they looked up. "Is it okay if I go for a ride in Levi's new car?"

Mom's head jerked back. "Not *this* again."

Dad wasn't going to get in the middle of anything. I could tell by the way his eyes darted away from mine and back to the business at hand—feeding Charity.

"But, Mom," I retorted. "He's a very good driver."

She grimaced. "Since when?"

"Since he . . . well, you know," I sputtered, trying to quickly remind them that Levi's wild horse-and-buggy days were over.

"Where is it you want to go?" she asked.

"Oh, down to the Dairy Queen or to get a soda somewhere." I sighed. "Levi and I *have* to talk, Mom. He's leaving for school in two weeks."

"Two weeks?" She stood up, beginning to clear the table.

"Please? We won't be gone long."

"Well, it's Saturday night, and you have plenty to do here at home to get ready for church tomorrow."

"So, can I go?"

She glanced at her watch. "Be home by nine-thirty."

"Yes!" I turned back to the phone. "Levi? I'll be ready in fifteen minutes," I said, trying not to let the excitement creep into my voice.

"*Gut,* Merry. I'll be by to pick you up at eight."

We said goodbye and hung up.

"Levi seems awfully persistent," Mom said, glancing up while loading the dishwasher.

"He's strong—goes after what he wants, but he knows when to back off, too," I said, sticking up for my friend. "That's what true love's all about, right? Knowing when to back off—to let go."

My remark was not well taken. But it got Dad's attention. "Sounds like you've been reading poetry again," he said, smiling. "But you're right. True love is patient and slow to act or react. Levi's been trained in the Scriptures all his life. He's seen love in action in the Amish community, that's for certain."

It struck me that Dad was taking Levi's side!

"Then you wouldn't mind if I agreed to be Levi's girl and wait for him while he goes to Bible school?" It was a test. I had to know what Dad would say.

Mom gasped a little in the background, but she remained silent while Dad burped the baby, talking to me. "Levi's girl, you say? Well, how do you feel about waiting around for him when you're only fourteen—"

"*Thirteen*," Mom interrupted. "She won't be fourteen until September." It was her standard response when it came to boys. *Too old for toys, too young for boys.* . . .

Dad jumped right in and began painting a dismal picture of high school and the many activities looming on the horizon of my freshman year. "Now, think of this, Mer. How would it be staying home and writing letters to Levi while your girlfriends are out with friends at football games and Homecoming parades?"

Dad had a point. He *always* did.

"I guess I'll just have to see if Levi wants to be tied down to a *thirteen*-year-old"—here I glanced at Mom, who caught the emphasis—"while he's off having a great time getting a taste of college life in the modern world."

"Levi's almost seventeen now," Mom offered. "There's a huge difference between being three years apart now and three years apart when you're in your twenties."

Once again, Mom was overexplaining. She was the commentator of the family and probably would've continued, but Charity let out a loud burp. Dad congratulated Charity, and Mom came rushing over to make sure she hadn't spit up on Dad's shirt.

"Have fun, Baby," I called to her, blowing a kiss. "I love you." And without offering to help with dishes, I headed upstairs to get my hair and face ready for the all-important chat with Levi.

When the doorbell rang, I waited for Dad to get it. He

liked to play host with Levi. They would sit in the living room and shoot the breeze for a while. Then in a few minutes, I'd come down. We'd had the same scenario twice before when Levi had come to take me for a walk.

I was standing at the top of the long main staircase, thinking it was about time to go down and make my appearance. The sun winked on the brass top of the banister, and I counted to ten.

The phone rang; someone picked it up downstairs. Then I heard Mom's voice floating up the back steps. "Merry, the phone's for you."

Not wanting to keep Levi waiting, I dashed down the hall to my parents' bedroom. "Hello?"

"Merry, Mistress of Mirth! I've missed many, many merry moments with you." It was Jon Klein, the Alliteration Wizard!

"Hi," I said. "You must be back from your vacation."

"Say that with all *b*'s," he said, laughing.

"I'd love to, but I really can't talk right now." What lousy timing!

"Let's see . . . likely not—Levi?"

*How'd he know?* I wondered.

"Well, actually, you're right. Levi's waiting downstairs." I wanted to be honest with him. "He and I have some things to discuss."

"Super-serious stuff?"

I paused to think. Jon's alliterating was bugging me—for the first time ever! "Could you stop talking that way and . . . and . . ."

"And what? What's wrong, Mer?" His voice was filled with question marks.

"I can't talk now, honest I can't," I said again. "Maybe I'll see you tomorrow."

"*Maybe?* You mean you're not coming to church?"

"I didn't mean that," I said. "I just meant—oh, never mind. Just forget it."

"Merry, wait." He sounded worried that I might hang up. "Can't we talk for a minute?"

"I'd like that," I said. "But I can't now. See ya."

His voice was still coming through the receiver as I held the phone in my hand, deciding whether or not to hang up. Then, feeling guilty, I brought the phone back up to my ear and listened.

"Merry? Are you still there?" he was asking.

"I'm here. Sorry."

"Hey, I called to invite you to the church potluck next weekend." His voice wavered a bit.

I was in shock. This was the first time Jon had formally asked me to anything. How long I had waited for this moment!

"So, what's it gonna be, Mistress Merry?"

My life was being ripped into pieces. Into thirds, actually. Jovial Jon, for one. And there was Levi—waiting downstairs to discuss our "future." Last, but certainly not least, a big chunk of my life was wrapped up in Charity, my precious sister-gift from God.

As I held the phone, I felt a distinct tugging in my heart. I couldn't even begin to respond. Jon was waiting for my answer. Levi was downstairs.

The next move was mine. Help!

# SIXTEEN

Mom was upstairs now. I could hear her across the hall, talking to Charity. Next thing I knew, she was waving developed film for Lissa in front of me.

I whispered, "Thanks," and put the photo-lab envelope on the bed. Mom left the room to attend to Charity.

"Uh . . . Jon," I said, glancing at my watch, "could I call you back later?"

"Like how late?"

"Sometime after nine-thirty." That's when I had to be home. And that's when I would know something about my status with Levi—and whether or not I was free to go with Jon to the church potluck.

"With watchful wonder, I'll await your call," he said.

I giggled. Jon was a real nut! Why had he waited so long to show an interest in me?

Downstairs, Levi looked truly dashing in his new T-shirt and jeans—without the usual suspenders. I wondered if he'd given them up, too.

Dad and Levi stood as I came into the room. "We

were just talking about you, Mer," Dad volunteered.

Levi nodded. "All good things." His eyes caught mine.

Suddenly, my cats showed up, sniffing at Levi's tennis shoes. "Okay, call off the cat squad," I teased, shooing the felines away. "Looks like they're still getting acquainted."

Levi grinned. "You'd think Lily White would know me by now, jah?"

I remembered the first time I'd seen Lily—in the hayloft last spring—before the Zooks' fire. Levi had called her a mouse-catcher. "Maybe she's worried you'll take her back to the barn," I said.

"Never again," Levi replied. Unfortunately, Lily White hadn't heard his remark. She was long gone. Probably outside with her adopted brothers.

"Well, I guess you two better be running along," Dad offered, rubbing his hands together.

"Nice chattin' with ya," Levi said to Dad, then shook his hand. I wondered if they'd come to some sort of gentlemen's agreement. It sure seemed fishy for them to be so chummy.

Levi followed me out through the wide archway and into the hall to the spacious entryway.

"Mom, I'm leaving," I called up the steps.

"Have fun," she called back.

Dad was leaning against the wide wood molding in the doorway leading to the living room. "Drive carefully" was all he said. Then with a wave, he smiled.

Outside, Levi walked around to the passenger side and opened the door for me. There was a spring in his step as he hurried to the driver's side after I was settled in. I admired the plush interior of his car. It still seemed odd to think that Levi actually owned modern wheels.

"Well, what do ya think?" he asked, jumping in behind the steering wheel.

"It's kind of strange. I'm used to seeing you with your horse, riding around in your Amish buggy."

He nodded. "I know whatcha mean." He looked at me for a second longer, then put the key into the ignition. "Are ya hungry?"

"We just ate, but thanks."

"Well, then, how 'bout a soda?" he suggested.

"Okay."

He switched on the radio to one of the local Christian stations, and we rode in silence down SummerHill Lane. At the turn-off to Hunsecker Road, Levi reached over and held my hand. My heart skipped a beat as he drove the familiar road to the old covered bridge.

"It's not gonna be easy sayin' goodbye, Merry," he said softly. "I want us to always be close like this—even when I'm gone to school."

I could hardly speak. The moment was filled with deep emotion. Levi slowed down as we approached Hunsecker Mill Bridge, and carefully he guided the car into the narrow, covered bridge. The loose planks rumbled under the wheels as we passed through.

"Do ya still wanna be my girl while I'm gone?" he asked as we headed out into the fading light of dusk. The sinking sun's red light cast a rosy glow over the road and trees as we headed for town.

I really couldn't decide. Not now . . . not with things

going so well between us. "What do *you* want, Levi?"

He smiled, his lips parting slightly. "Remember our talk in the gazebo a few weeks ago?"

"I remember," I said, feeling terribly shy.

"Well, I haven't changed my mind about anything. But you're still very young and . . ." He paused. "And there's something else. I feel I've received a call from the Lord, ya know. A call into the ministry."

"That should come first," I replied.

By the time we got to McDonald's and went through the drive-through, Levi had pretty much come to his own conclusion about us. I was glad he was the one deciding, but very sad that he wouldn't be around SummerHill after August thirteenth.

"I hope you'll write now and again," he said, glancing at me. "I don't wanna lose you, Merry. But it just wouldn't be fair to tie you down. Not now."

I thought back to what Dad had said at supper. If I hadn't known better, I would've thought he'd given Levi the same spiel he'd given me.

"Of course I'll write," I said, pushing the straw into the plastic lid. "And you'll be back to visit the farm, won't you?"

"Jah," he said. "Curly John and Sarah's baby will be comin' soon, don't forget. So I'll be back."

"Rachel says the baby's due in November."

He nodded. "Sarah's been busy makin' all kinds of booties and things."

His reference to booties got me sidetracked, thinking about Charity back home. "I bet Sarah's excited."

"Jah. She talks about namin' the baby after me if it's

a boy." Levi was obviously delighted.

"And what if the baby's a girl—then what'll they name her?" I turned to look at the familiar face, tanned from the sun, rugged from the elements.

"My brother wants her to be named for Sarah."

"Curly John chose Sarah's name?"

Levi nodded.

"How sweet—baby Sarah Zook," I said, trying the name on for fun. "How will you tell her name apart from her mother's?"

"The Amish love nicknames," Levi chuckled. "She'll hafta have one fer sure." Then he surprised me and asked about Charity. "How's that little one ya had yesterday . . . in the basket, ya know?"

I hoped Rachel hadn't told him about her being abandoned. She'd promised. "Oh, she's fine," I said.

"That's gut," he said. "Funny, though, I was sure I saw the same baby—same basket—in town with Miss Spindler yesterday afternoon."

I swallowed hard. "Really?"

"I'm certain of it." For a few moments only the radio broke the stillness. "What do ya make of it?"

"Guess she was baby-sitting," I said. Would Dad want me to tell more? I didn't think so.

"It's awful strange—Old Hawk Eyes with a baby." Levi made the left turn onto SummerHill Lane. "Who would've thought the old lady would wanna go shoppin' with a baby?"

The same question had crossed my mind. But that was before I'd come to realize how very kind, even nurturing, our neighbor lady was. "I guess when you know a person long enough . . . well, eventually the hidden secrets of their personality are revealed."

Levi looked at me. "Now ya sound like a philosopher."

We laughed together, sharing the memorable moment as honeysuckle aroma wafted through the windows of Levi's beautiful car.

"I'm glad I know ya, Merry," he said, grinning. "Do I know all the secret parts of yer personality yet?"

I kept a straight face. "I doubt it."

More laughter.

When Levi pulled into my driveway at nine-thirty on the dot, I could only think of one thing: He was leaving SummerHill. Things would never be the same between us.

"Why so glum?" he asked.

I forced a smile. "You know me, I hate change. It's always hard for me."

"Jah." He nodded. "But it's a new beginning for me. And fer ya, too, Merry. You'll be goin' to high school."

I nodded, not wild about the prospect of leaving my old middle school behind to start over in a brand-new place.

"We'll still see each other," Levi said. "I promise ya that."

Something inside me secretly wished he was making another kind of promise, even though I knew he was right about us going our separate ways.

He held tightly to the steering wheel, looking straight ahead. "Yer a wonderful girl, Merry. I've known it since the day ya saved me from drownin' in the pond behind the house."

I wasn't sure why he always had to bring that up. Was it the saving of his life that meant so much to him? Or was it me, myself?

Just then, Abednego, my fat, black cat, jumped up onto the hood of the car. He arched his back and hissed.

Levi leaned back in his seat and burst out laughing.

I got out of the car. "Abednego, you crazy cat. Come here!" I tried several coaxing tactics on him, but he refused to come.

By now Levi was outside, too, still getting a kick out of the way Abednego was misbehaving. I apologized for my rude cat, and instead of continuing to persuade and coax, I left Abednego behind and walked with Levi to the front porch.

"Still coming tomorrow to Faithie's graveside?" I asked as we stood at the door.

"I'll be there."

"I'm glad," I said. "Thanks for the soda."

He took my hand and held it in both of his. "I'll be missin' ya, Merry."

"I'll miss you, too, Levi." We said good-night, knowing full well there were two more weeks—wonderful summer days and nights—before Levi had to go.

Yet the sadness stayed with me. It stayed long after his gleaming white Mustang pulled out of the driveway and sped down SummerHill.

# SEVENTEEN

I headed upstairs to my room. The events of the night had come as somewhat of a relief, yet I was still dealing with mixed emotions about Levi. Mostly sad ones. So sad that I completely forgot about Jon Klein and my promise to call.

Charity started to cry and I hurried to her room. "What's the matter with you, sweetie?" I asked, picking her up.

Mom came running. "I wonder why she's fussy," she remarked. "I just finished bathing her, and I was sure she was asleep for the night."

"She just wanted to see her big sister, that's all." I walked around the makeshift nursery, hugging her close. "Isn't that right?"

Mom sat in the rocking chair and watched me. "There have been some new developments," she said.

I perked up my ears. "When? While I was gone? What?"

"Whoa, Merry, slow down." She was smiling. "There's nothing to worry about. In fact, it's very good news."

"Really?" I moved closer to Mom, eager to hear.

"The authorities have located Charity's parents somewhere in Virginia. They're in jail now. Fortunately, they have signed away—relinquished—all parental rights."

"Yes! This is truly amazing."

Charity babbled as I bent down and kissed her tiny cheek. "You're gonna be ours forever!" I danced around the room, rejoicing.

"By noon Monday, we'll have legal custody—temporarily, of course. It takes time to finalize adoptions."

"You're kidding—she's actually going to be up for adoption?" This was too good to be true.

Mom nodded. "Your dad and I agree that we want you and Skip to be involved in the final decision." She smiled, wiping a tear off her cheek. "We had a long talk about it tonight. We dearly love Charity and are willing to start over, so to speak. Things could be very lonely for all of us come fall when Skip's gone. A baby . . . a baby like Charity would be a welcome addition to our family."

"So, what's to decide?" I said. Charity was going to be ours! She was going to stay right here and grow up with doting parents and a sister who adored her. I couldn't believe God had answered my prayer so quickly.

"We want to have Charity here with us for a full week before we make our final decision," Mom said. "It's best to pray in earnest about something this important."

"I've already prayed," I said, referring to the prayer in the cellar three days ago. "God came through for me. Charity stays."

Jon met me at the door leading to our Sunday school class. "I waited last night for you to call," he said without the typical alliteration routine. "What happened?"

"I'm sorry. Maybe we should talk after class," I replied, heading inside, looking for an empty chair.

Jon followed, asking if he could sit with me just as Mrs. Simms, our teacher, stood up to welcome the visitors. "What about the potluck? Did you decide?" Jon whispered.

"Sure, I'll go," I answered, feeling slightly disloyal to Levi. I tried to dismiss the thought. After all, he and I were only friends now. It was okay for me to like lots of different boys. Still, the idea of hanging out with Jon while Levi was off at the concert in Ephrata alone bothered me.

After class, I gave the package of pictures to Lissa. "They turned out great," I said as she opened them.

"Wow, you're right." She looked at each picture. "Grammy will be so excited to get these. How much do I owe you?"

I gave her the receipt. "Here, you can pay me later."

"Mom'll write you a check after church, okay?" Her wavy hair was pulled back in a perky blue bow. And I noticed that as we talked, she glanced at Jon several times.

"Glad you like them." I turned to go. Jon was waiting in the hallway.

"Like them? They're the best pictures I've ever had taken," Lissa said, following me out to the hall. "You're such a good photographer, Mer."

"Thanks," I said.

Lissa stood beside me while I hung out with Jon and

our pastor's daughter, Ashley Horton, who just so happened to like the Alliteration Wizard, too.

"Well, who's coming to the potluck next weekend?" Ashley asked, looking around.

"Merry and I are," Jon stated, grinning at me.

Lissa acted cool, not showing her surprise. But Ashley stood there and yakked about how much fun the potluck would be. I wondered when she would stop talking.

That's when Mom came down the hall, Charity and diaper bag in tow. Apparently, she was headed for the nursery.

"Oh, Mom, let me show off my new sister," I said, taking Charity from her. "We can't put her in the nursery on her very first Sunday with us. I can hold her in church, and if she gets fussy, I'll come out and walk around with her."

Mom agreed and headed off to save a seat for me upstairs in the sanctuary.

Lissa looked shocked as she and Ashley crowded in, touching Charity's little hands and soft, chubby cheeks. "This is your *sister*?" Lissa asked.

"Well . . . she will be soon. We hope."

Lissa looked confused.

"It's about what I couldn't say the other night on the phone. Remember?" I tried to explain, sounding rather vague. "Evidently, the stranger we saw in the pickup was looking for a place to hide a baby."

"How cruel," Ashley said. "She's so tiny. How could someone do that?"

"It's awful, that's what it is," Lissa whispered. "She's so precious."

They had lots of questions, but the organ was starting to play and it was time for church. Jon waited around as though he wanted to sit with me. "Would it be all right with your parents?" he asked as we headed for the stairs.

"If you don't mind sitting in a pew with a two-month-old."

He smiled. "Do babies bite?"

I laughed, delighted with Jon's attention.

❧　　❧

Surprisingly, Charity slept through most of the pastor's sermon. "Love wasn't put in your heart to stay," he quoted. "Love isn't love till you give it away." Then he read his Scripture text. "First Corinthians chapter thirteen, verses four and five. 'Love is patient, love is kind. It does not envy, it does not boast, it is not proud. It is not rude, it is not self-seeking, it is not easily angered, it keeps no record of wrongs.' Today, I want to focus on the passage, 'love is not self-seeking.' Love that is freely given is Godlike love."

I listened intently, thinking off and on of Levi, who had declared his love for me weeks ago but who refused to cling to it—releasing me for now. He'd exhibited the selfless kind of love the pastor was talking about.

After the service, Jon asked more questions about the baby. "Where did you find her?"

"It was wild, really. I thought at first I heard my kitten crying, but when I searched, I discovered this baby in our gazebo!"

He was as surprised as everyone else. My parents' friends gathered around oohing and aahing over the baby.

I gave her to Mom, who held her up for her friends to see. People just couldn't seem to get enough of our pudgy darling.

"You picked the perfect name for a pretty petite person," Jon said, beginning his irresistible word game. He smiled, egging me on. "Your turn."

"Charity? Chalk it up as a chapter in a changed heart."

Jon was clapping. "Exceptionally excellent example!"

"Thank you . . . I think." We were in glossary glory.

᙮     ᙮

After dinner, Mom, Dad, and I, along with Charity, took the short ride down SummerHill to the small cemetery where gravestones lay scattered in rows across a tree-lined meadow. Levi's car was parked nearby, and Dad mentioned how thoughtful it was that he had come.

"It was Levi's idea," I said.

"What a really terrific kid," Mom said, handing Charity to Dad. "Too bad he has to go off to school so soon."

I wondered about her statement. Just last night she seemed to be opposed to my spending time with Levi.

"Hullo, Doctor Hanson," Levi said, catching up with Dad. He spied the baby, and a shadow of surprise crept across his handsome face.

"It's good of you to come," Dad said.

Levi stared at the baby.

"Baby Charity's going to be staying with us," I explained quietly as we fell into step together. "It's a long story."

"Ach jah," he said, and I knew I'd have to level with

him about Miss Spindler sooner or later.

*Love is kind.*

Solemnly, we approached Faithie's white gravestone. The rolling hills around us were ablaze with color. Yellow daisies bloomed everywhere. Levi went with me to gather some for Faithie's grave. It was part of our family tradition. The celebration of her life.

Finally, all of us held hands and sang *Amazing Grace.* Levi's clear voice rang out, and a lump rose in my throat as I thought of him leaving. Purposely, I stared at the words etched on Faithie's gravestone. *Faith Hanson, precious daughter and dear sister, in heaven with our Lord.*

Levi had been fond of Faithie, too. Not in the same way as he loved me. But he *had* loved her. The Zook kids were Faithie's and my favorite playmates in a predominantly Amish area. Faithie and I loved spending time with our plain friends—skating on the pond in winter, riding in the pony cart in the springtime, playing volleyball barefoot in summer . . . and then there was the hayloft. That wonderful, almost magical place high in the two-story "bank barn." All this and much more, Faithie and I had shared with Levi and his brothers and sisters. We'd practically grown up beyond the willow grove—on the Zook farm.

I choked back the tears as Dad prayed that our hearts would be tender to the love each of us shared, neighbor and family member alike. "And may we always remember that our days on this earth are numbered," he prayed. "That we ought to treasure every minute we have as a family until you call us home. Amen."

I wiped the tears from my eyes as we turned to head

down the hill to the car. Dad was right. I knew in my heart that if I could do it all again—relive those seven short years with Faithie—I would be more careful to cherish every minute.

*Love never fails.*

When we arrived home, Rachel was waiting on the front porch. She looked pale, and as I got out of the car and ran toward her, I noticed her eyes were red and swollen.

"Rachel, what's wrong?"

"It's Sarah's baby. . . ." She put her hands to her face, covering her eyes. "Sarah's gone to the hospital."

"Why? What happened?" Fear gripped me.

Rachel shook her head, unable to speak.

Dad stopped to talk with her while Mom took Charity into the house for her nap. "Is your sister-in-law having premature labor?" he asked.

Rachel shook her head. "It can't be—it's only her fifth month."

Dad's eyes showed concern. "I'll leave for the hospital right away." He touched Rachel's shoulder.

"Thanks, Dad," I said as he hurried into the house.

*Love is patient.*

The wait was terribly long. Rachel stayed at our house until it was time for the afternoon milking. Before she left, I hugged her. "We'll be praying," I said. "And if we don't hear something soon, I'll ask Mom to page Dad."

She nodded. "*Da Herr sei mit du.* The Lord be with you." Off she ran down the lane toward the shortcut to the farm, through the willows.

"And with *you*, Rachel!" I called after my friend.

# EIGHTEEN

The phone did not ring until almost seven. When I picked it up, I detected the sadness in Dad's voice. "Sarah lost her baby."

My heart sank. "I'll run and tell Rachel. She's waiting to know . . . her parents, too."

"Tell them Sarah's resting now," Dad said. "She's being sedated."

I could not imagine what poor Sarah and Curly John were experiencing. They were young—newlyweds—just two years older than Skip. And this was their first little one. Now Baby Zook was gone. Gone to heaven too soon.

I ran upstairs and sat on the floor beside the cradle that had been mine. Sadly, I looked down at Charity, now sound asleep. "Nothing must ever happen to you," I said out of sheer determination. "I won't let it. I won't! You're ours forever."

*Love always protects.*

Charity stirred sweetly in her sleep, unaware of the turmoil in my heart.

On Monday morning, Mom and Dad went to town with Charity to do the paper work for temporary custody. I stayed home and took pictures outside. The gazebo was the setting this time. With the news of Sarah's miscarriage fresh in my mind, I created several scenes using Faithie's pine cradle. I didn't mean it to be morbid, but maybe it was.

Anyway, I had my own unique way of working through my sorrow over Sarah and Curly John's loss. By combining the gazebo with the empty cradle, I was bringing three factors together: my own pain at losing Faithie, Sarah's recent loss, and the discovery of Charity—the love I was clinging to. What great joy she'd brought to me! And now to my family.

Mom had made things quite clear, however. By this time Friday, we were to make a final decision about Charity. Mom had said to pray about it. I had. There was nothing left to say. I wanted Charity—wanted her forever.

As I ran around the gazebo, taking this shot and that from various angles, I remembered Dad's words. *True love is patient and slow to act or react.*

I must admit, I'd gotten caught up in the emotion of the moment, letting baby fever run away with me. But when it came right down to it—to the everyday, day-in-day-out schedule of having a baby to care for, well . . . I could see Mom's point. I was *not* the one most involved. She was.

Was I being selfish wanting this baby?

*Love is not self-seeking.*

I stopped to adjust the aperture, the lens opening, for correct lighting. Then I heard someone walking toward me and turned to see who it was. "Rachel, hi!"

"Whatcha doin'?" she asked.

I knew she'd spotted the cradle. It was the focal point of the gazebo picture—how could she miss it?

"Oh, just taking some pictures."

She was quiet for a moment, her eyes downcast. We sat on the gazebo steps while the cats came and rubbed up against our bare ankles.

Carefully, I put my camera back into its case and snapped it shut. Looking up, I saw that Rachel's eyes were bright with tears. "You're crying!"

She brushed her cheek with the back of her hand. "I'm sad for Sarah. She's brokenhearted, Merry. And there's been some very bad news."

My throat turned to cotton. "What is it?"

"The doctor says, like as not, Sarah will never be able to have children." A sad little sigh burst from her lips.

"Oh, Rachel . . . I'm so sorry." I put my arm around her, sharing her pain. Her light brown hair was wrapped up in a thick bun at the back of her head and covered by the white netting she always wore. Her shoulders shook as she wept. I'd never seen her cry so hard. Not even at her grandfather's funeral.

We sat there together under the towering leafy maples, and I comforted Rachel as best I could. At last, she dried her eyes. "Ya know, you're my best friend, Cousin Merry."

"I am?" I was startled by her words.

Her eyes widened. "Ain't I yours?"

I'd never thought of Rachel that way—only Faithie. But now that she mentioned it, I guessed she was right.

"Oh, Rachel . . ." I hugged her hard. "You're the best friend I could ever have."

She smiled through her tears, standing up suddenly. "I hafta go help Mam out with choppin' carrots and celery—we're makin' chow chow."

I sat there clinging to my cats as she dashed across the side yard and headed for SummerHill Lane. She'd called me her best friend. I shouldn't have been so surprised. Rachel and I had shared everything. Always had. And now this—the loss of her brother's baby.

In spite of the sadness, I felt consoled and heartened. It was truly amazing—even without Faithie, I'd had a best friend all these years!

❧    ❧

Later, Shadrach and Meshach followed me as I went into the house to put away my camera equipment. I went back to the gazebo to retrieve the cradle. There on the wooden floor, I spotted the safety pin—the one that had pinned the note to Charity's pink blanket. I stopped to pick it up, turning it over in my hand.

A startling realization hit me. The note had pleaded for my help. *Please take care of me and love me as your own.* And Merry Hanson, the problem-solver, had decided to do just that. That was me—Miss Fix-It.

Dad had recognized the trait in me early on, and Skip constantly teased me about taking in strays. Cats, people . . . I'd even risked my life to save Lily White—a mouse-catcher, of all things. And now, my latest attempt at saving the world was a two-month-old baby!

Things were becoming clear, making sense. I understood why Mom and Dad had asked me to pray about the decision. They were absolutely right. A decision to make Charity my baby sister was far too important to simply choose out of emotion.

I scooped up Lily White and stuffed her into the bib pocket of my overalls. "C'mon, you. We're going for a walk. Just the two of us." And down the lane I went.

Four days had passed since Mom and I sat together in the willow grove talking about life and love and God's will. I wanted to go there now. To be alone. So much had happened since Thursday, and the events were beginning to overwhelm me.

Lily White must've sensed my tension. She kept meowing and trying to wrestle out of my wide pocket. "No, no. You stay in there, little girl," I said, holding her gently in place.

She fought me, trying to break free.

Frustrated, I shouted, "You're staying right here!"

The poor little fluff of white recoiled, hiding in the pocket seam. *Mew*, she replied.

"Oh, baby, I'm sorry," I said, kneeling down on the worn, narrow path, stroking her head. "I do love you. Honest. I just want you to stay where it's safe, where I can take care of you. Don't you see?"

When I took my hands away, Lily White clawed her way out of my overalls and ran off. I hurried after her, calling for her to return. "Come back, Lily! Please! I'm sorry."

But Lily had other ideas. She skittered through the willows and down toward the meadow where the cows were grazing. Had she seen a mouse?

"Lily!" She ignored me, obviously wanting her freedom. I'd clung too tightly to her.

Crouching on the soft ground under the biggest willow in the grove, I felt as though the world was sitting on my shoulder. The secret place was nearly enclosed with green branches and tendrils, forming a canopy over my head. "Come back, Lily," I cried. "I love you too much to let you wander away. I want you with *me*."

When I stopped crying, I realized how selfish my words were. How selfish I was in other ways, too. I'd clung selfishly to Faithie's memory, blocking out close friendships and letting the obsession with it come between Mom and me. And I'd thought *she* had a problem!

*Love keeps no record of wrongs.*

And there was Charity. I didn't have to think twice to know the truth. I was being selfish about her, too.

A young Amish couple had heard sorrowful words yesterday upon the loss of their first baby: no birth children for them—ever!

What was it Rachel had said last week?—that it would be a terrible heartache for an Amish wife to be without children.

*Love is not self-seeking.*

Me, me—that's all I could think about these days. *My* sister, *my* baby . . .

Leaping up, I parted some of the heavy branches, letting the hot sun beat down on my face. "Forgive me, Lord," I said simply. "Help me put the pastor's sermon into practice. Give me the kind of love that doesn't cling for dear life, because love isn't love till *I* give it away."

Though I was hot and beginning to perspire, the sun's

rays encompassed me. They were like the light of God's love pouring into my soul. Shining the Father's torch of truth.

I let go of the branches and slipped into the shadowy coolness of the willow grove. A rustling came from behind, and startled, I turned to look.

"Merry, don't be frightened."

"Mom, what are you doing here?" I ran to her, careful not to awaken Charity, who was sleeping in her wicker basket. She smiled, glancing at the baby. "I thought it was time for our little one to be formally introduced to your secret place."

I nodded. "Doesn't look like she cares too much about it right now." I looked around, enjoying the moment and feeling freer than I had in years. "We have to talk," I said. "With Dad."

Mom's eyes grew serious. "Oh?"

I breathed in a deep breath, my heart pounding. "It's about keeping Charity."

# NINETEEN

We didn't stay long in the willow grove. The sparse clouds of morning had thickened and were beginning to grow dark. A clap of thunder crackled in our ears as we hurried in the back door.

"We made it just in time," Mom said, uncovering Charity, who was wide awake now and moving her little arms excitedly.

"When will Dad be home?" I asked, staring at the baby.

"Probably late."

I was disappointed. "After supper?"

"I'm afraid so." Mom took Charity out of the basket and handed her to me. "Will you change her, please? I have some calls to make."

I wondered what Mom was up to but didn't ask. She seemed rather preoccupied. Maybe she was thinking about what I'd said in the willows. I was tempted to tiptoe down the hall and eavesdrop. One little snatch of conversation might give me a clue.

Slowly, I inched toward the main staircase. The door to the study was partly open, and I stood there listening.

"Before you come home," Mom was saying, "can you touch base with your contacts at the Department of Social Services?"

Silence on her end. Was she talking to Dad?

Then—"I'm not sure. But check and see what must be done." It sounded as though she was about to hang up, so I scooted away from the door and carried Charity upstairs.

I wondered how Mom and Dad would feel about giving up Charity for Curly John and Sarah Zook. Of course, it was a bit premature to be thinking that way, especially since Sarah was still in the hospital and had no knowledge of our little Charity.

Torn between wanting to keep Charity and wanting to help soothe the pain for Sarah and Curly John, I played with the darling baby who'd brought us so much delight—singing and saying the nursery rhymes Faithie and I had learned. I'd grown so attached to this baby. Just thinking about taking her to live with someone else made me half sick.

And what about Mom? She loved Charity, too. How would *she* feel? And Dad? Anyone could see how charmed he was by the baby.

I changed Charity's diaper and carried her back downstairs. Mom was busily stirring up something in the kitchen. She didn't even glance up as I strolled into the family room with Charity. Sometimes Mom worked out her stress in her cooking. This afternoon was one of those times, I was sure. If I was correct, it was best to steer clear.

I found the remote and scanned the TV channels

while sitting in Dad's easy chair. The news was on all the major networks. A ballet was on public television. I switched it back to the local news. One of the leading stories was about couples and infertility drugs. I hoped Sarah and Curly John weren't watching, then I remembered they didn't believe in having a television or anything else electrical in their house—probably had it turned off in the hospital, too.

I held Charity up in my arms, gazing into her eyes. "How would you like to grow up Amish? You'd never have to worry about eating junk food. Nope. You'd have fresh fruits and vegetables and lots of rich milk to drink."

She cooed a little.

"I really wish your first mama and daddy had loved you more," I surprised myself by saying. "But don't worry. You have a heavenly Father who cared enough to send you here so we could find you a terrific home."

Mom peeked her head around the corner. "Is that you talking, Mer?"

I smiled. "Charity and I are having a sisterly chat."

"Just checking," she said and left.

"Now, where were we?" I touched her soft cheek. "Oh yes. I think I might've already found some parents for you. They don't know about it, though. When Dad comes home tonight, we'll discuss it." I stopped talking and listened to her sweet gurgling sounds.

"Merry, if the doorbell rings, will you let Miss Spindler in?" Mom called from the kitchen.

"Miss Spindler's coming over?"

"She wants to see the baby again," she answered.

"Okay."

Soon I heard Mom going upstairs. Had she called Old Hawk Eyes? I certainly hadn't heard the phone ring.

Feeling a bit gloomy, I thought back to the first night Charity and I had spent together. "You're mighty little to have already experienced your first sleepover. And outside, too. . . ." I remembered Faithie's insistence on sleeping outside with me in the gazebo so long ago.

The doorbell rang, putting an end to my reverie. I peeked out through the curtains. It was Miss Spindler, all right. Dressed to the hilt, as usual.

"Come in," I said, opening the screen door. "Mom was expecting you."

"I've made some more outfits for Charity." Her voice was softer than I'd ever heard it. She looked down at the baby in my arms as though she'd just seen an angel. "My, oh, my, if she hasn't grown in just two days."

I smiled, leading her into the family room, where she sat in the rocker nearest the window. I knew she was eager to hold the baby, so I relinquished Charity and went to get some iced tea for our guest. While I was in the kitchen, I poked my head into the stairwell leading upstairs. "Mom, Miss Spindler's here."

"I'll be right down," she said. "Make her some iced tea, will you?"

I congratulated myself on thinking ahead. Mom's hostess mentality was beginning to rub off, it seemed.

"Here we are," I said to Miss Spindler, the way Mom always did.

"Why, thank you, dear." She placed the glass on the windowsill, gently rocking. "I heard tell that young Sarah and Curly John had an unfortunate event happen just yesterday."

"It's very sad," I replied, pulling up a chair.

"Seems to me, they'd be needing some cheering up."

I nodded. "I'd like to visit Sarah when she gets home from the hospital."

"Well, I was thinking the very same thing. And while we're at it"—and here she lowered her voice—"why don't we take Charity along for an outing? You know, she absolutely loved riding in that little car seat I bought."

I wondered about Miss Spindler's comment. Was she thinking of the baby—getting her out for a ride—or was she thinking of Sarah? Then I wondered right out loud. "What do you think about Sarah holding a baby—you know, Charity? Do you think it would comfort her, or would it make her feel worse?"

A surprising thing happened as I looked into Ruby Spindler's face. Her eyes filled with tears, and her face . . . her face began to shine with sheer joy. "Oh, Merry, you have no idea what holding this baby would do for the poor girl. Why, let me tell you something, dear."

Mom had crept in as Miss Spindler was talking, but she held her finger to her lips as the old woman continued.

"For as long as I remember, I've longed for a child. Of course, not being a married lady made it quite impossible, from my way of thinking. But when I first set eyes on this here youngster," she glanced lovingly at Charity, now wide awake. "I knew that I would be made whole if I could just hold her in my arms. It was as Simeon of old, who longed to see the Christ child. He knew that he would not die until he held the baby Jesus in his arms and blessed Him."

I listened, truly amazed.

"Yes, my dear, this baby, abandoned and alone in the world, has brought great comfort to my heart." She sighed, touching Charity's hand. "And I do believe she'll do the same for poor, hurting Sarah."

Mom's eyes filled with tears, and when I looked up she didn't try to hide them as they spilled down her cheeks. Mom agreed with Miss Spindler. I knew it by the tender look on her face. It wouldn't be long before we'd be taking baby Charity on a very special outing—to visit Sarah Zook.

# TWENTY

I was sound asleep when Dad arrived home from his late shift at the hospital. He was dressed and gone before dawn the next morning, so I knew our talk would have to wait several more days.

In the meantime, Mom gave her consent for Miss Spindler to take Charity and me to visit Sarah Zook. Rachel wanted to come along, too, so the four of us squeezed into the jazzy red sports car bright and early Friday morning. Rachel sat up in the bucket seat next to Old Hawk Eyes, while I sat in the back next to Charity in her infant seat.

"How's Sarah doing?" I asked Rachel.

She turned around and looked through the wide opening between the seats. "Sarah's a strong, healthy girl. She was out helping Curly John yesterday in the field."

"Really?" I was glad to hear it.

"Her body's doin' fine, but her heart, well that's a whole 'nother story." Rachel's eyes told the truth. "She's a-hurtin' and nothin'—no one—can make the pain stop."

Miss Spindler glanced at Rachel. "She knows we're coming, though, right?"

Rachel nodded. "I told her Merry was baby-sittin'

and would it be all right to bring the baby along."

"And what did she say to that?" Miss Spindler seemed too eager.

Rachel shrugged. "Oh, she didn't mind. She was just glad to hear that company was comin'."

"Company, eh?" Miss Spindler cackled. And I knew she had something up her sleeve.

❧   ❧

Sarah looked a bit pale when she answered the front door. "Wilkom," she said, noticing the baby immediately. "Come and sit."

I carried Charity inside in her infant seat. Miss Spindler directed me to unbuckle her and take her out promptly. "How would you like to be cooped up in one of them there things?" She waved her hand at it, as though she thought it served no purpose.

Happily, I did as I was told. Being close to Charity—with her nestled in my arms—was the best place to be.

Evidently, Miss Spindler felt the same way. No sooner had I settled into one of Sarah's hickory rockers, when here came Ruby cooing and carrying on. "Let me hold the little angel," she said.

Sarah leaned forward, her eyes riveted. "Ach, what a perty baby!"

Rachel, sitting next to Sarah, nodded. "And she's *gut*, too, jah?" Rachel remarked.

I smiled. "I think she must be the best baby I've ever taken care of."

"Believe you me, this here little one is a gift straight from the throne of God," Miss Spindler said. I could tell she meant every word, too. Her eyes beamed as she smiled at Charity.

We chatted with Sarah, talking about the weather and asking about her quilting projects. It was hard not to notice the baby things scattered around the living room, which was as sparsely furnished as most Old Order Amish front rooms.

It broke my heart to see the large, handmade cradle in the corner of the room. I wondered why someone hadn't put it away. A cradle! What a sad reminder to the young husband and wife. Sad and sorrowful. I had a powerful urge to get up and hide it in the attic!

Sarah stood up, motioning to Rachel. "Wouldja like a piece of pie—black raspberry? I just made it fresh before ya came."

"I'd love a piece," Miss Spindler said, glancing at me.

"Sounds good, thanks," I said.

While Sarah and Rachel were out in the kitchen, Miss Spindler turned Charity over on her tummy, laying her across her lap. "She likes the world upside-down this way," she said. "I think it helps get the gas off her tummy."

I had no idea where Miss Spindler had picked up all these tips on baby care. But it touched my heart, seeing Charity so loved by the old woman. A lonely, old woman. How we had misunderstood her!

Sarah carried a tray of dishes filled with large servings of raspberry pie for each of us. When she came to Miss Spindler, whose lap was plum full with Charity, Sarah offered to hold the baby. "Ya need some space to enjoy yer pie," she said.

I grinned. It was the very thing Ruby Spindler had

hoped for. Her expression gave her away, and I knew the true reason why we'd come to see Sarah today.

❧    ❧

Dad was waiting for our talk when I arrived home with Charity. "How was your visit with Sarah?" he asked.

"She seems better, I think."

Mom took the baby from me and kissed her. "We hoped Sarah's seeing little Charity wouldn't upset her unduly."

I sat on the green paisley sofa next to Dad. "You probably won't believe it—I know *I* didn't."

"What do you mean?" Mom held Charity close. It was as though she were holding her breath as well.

"Charity was just what the doctor ordered," I said, using Miss Spindler's expression. "Sarah literally fell in love with our baby." I realized what I'd said. "Uh . . . I mean, *the* baby."

Dad caught on, and rubbing his chin said, "Your mother tells me you've been wanting to talk about that."

I was determined to go through with it—my change of heart. And after today, after I'd witnessed the transformation in Sarah Zook, I knew I'd have the courage to spell it out for Dad. For Mom, too.

"To begin with, I've been awfully selfish. About lots of things around here. But most of all about the baby. Neither of you know it, but last week I prayed a very selfish prayer. When I found Charity in the gazebo, I just assumed she was meant for me . . . for us."

Dad folded his hands, giving me his undivided attention. "Don't be too hard on yourself, Mer. You're just a kid."

"Dad!"

"In *my* book you are." He squeezed my elbow. "Go on."

I stared at Charity, who was waving her tiny fists the way she had the night I found her. "Everyone loves this baby. And everyone who sees her wants to get their hands on her—to adopt her."

Dad nodded thoughtfully.

"You and Mom—what do you want to do about adopting Charity?"

Mom spoke up. "We've been thinking and praying all week about it."

"So have I," I said, remembering my experience in the willow grove.

"And what have you decided?" Dad asked. "We want your input as well."

I was hesitant to just blurt it out. Mom had overheard Miss Spindler talking with me—the day she revealed how Charity had comforted her. Made her feel whole somehow. Mom had cried at the old woman's sentiments.

"As hard as it would be to give Charity up, I think it's the right thing to do. There are couples waiting—women who can't have babies. Hurting people . . ." I couldn't go on. It was too hard to sit here in the same room as my little foster sister and talk about giving her away.

"We've been thinking the same thing," Mom said softly.

I was relieved.

It was Dad's turn. "The Lord's been good to your

mother and me—giving us three beautiful babies—and having the blessing of seeing two of them grow up." He didn't continue, but it was what he left unsaid that spoke loudest.

Charity would be dearly loved here, but when another family was approved and ready, she would leave us. She would bring love to a couple whose waiting arms were empty.

The next day was the church potluck. We dressed Charity up in one of my old sunsuits with a lace-trimmed sun hat to match. She was the object of everyone's affection. Even Jon Klein enjoyed talking to her in alliteration-eze. In fact, he and I played our word game until the cows came home. Actually, there were no cows on the church grounds—it's one of those silly things people say around here.

And Charity? Things *did* work out for her to go live with Curly John and Sarah. Thanks to Dad's arranging it. They had to have a home study, a caseworker, and a financial statement for Social Services, but when it was finally all said and done, they were the happiest little couple this side of the Conestoga River.

I was mighty happy myself. After all, there aren't many baby-sitters around who'll work for nothing. And that's just what I did. Offered my services to the sweetest baby on SummerHill.

Miss Spindler was elated. She kept making crocheted outfits and booties to match. Perhaps too many, but you couldn't stop her. She was a giver, I'd discovered. And give, she did!

Skip finally came home from camp, packed up, and left for college. He was fine with the decision to let Charity go.

Now the house is empty . . . and quiet. Sometimes too quiet. But I'm finding ways to fill it with noise. Like the sleepovers Lissa and I have planned.

As for Lissa's grammy, she's coming to Lancaster in October. Wants me to take pictures of her when the leaves turn. She's insisting on paying for my services, which she thought looked mighty professional. Maybe between baby-sitting and picture-taking, I'll have enough experience to land a real job. In the meantime, I'm writing letters to Levi and getting good at Jon's alliteration word game.

Charity started rolling over and trying to say, "Mam," which is what the Amish call their mothers. Her name's been legally changed to Mary Zook. The first name's for me, except no Amish family would ever spell it M-e-r-r-y. But it's an honor to have the baby of my dreams with a given name that *sounds* like mine.

Now, if I could just get Lily White to stop making noise like a newborn baby when she cries! And by the way, I'm working on the Miss Fix-It label. I'm going to try to be more content with what I have—with what God's given me. It's a new beginning.

So is being a freshman at James Buchanan High. It's unbelievable what happened when I entered a photography contest. Who would've thought that Ashley Horton and I would go head to head over a silly contest—*and* the Alliteration Wizard—in the same month!

But that's another story. . . .

# Also by Beverly Lewis

## PICTURE BOOKS

Cows in the House    Annika's Secret Wish
Just Like Mama

## THE CUL-DE-SAC KIDS
### Children's Fiction

| | |
|---|---|
| The Double Dabble Surprise | Tarantula Toes |
| The Chicken Pox Panic | Green Gravy |
| The Crazy Christmas Angel Mystery | Backyard Bandit Mystery |
| No Grown-ups Allowed | Tree House Trouble |
| Frog Power | The Creepy Sleep-Over |
| The Mystery of Case D. Luc | The Great TV Turn-Off |
| The Stinky Sneakers Mystery | Piggy Party |
| Pickle Pizza | The Granny Game |
| Mailbox Mania | Mystery Mutt |
| The Mudhole Mystery | Big Bad Beans |
| Fiddlesticks | The Upside-Down Day |
| The Crabby Cat Caper | The Midnight Mystery |

## ABRAM'S DAUGHTERS
### Adult Fiction

The Covenant

## THE HERITAGE OF LANCASTER COUNTY
### Adult Fiction

The Shunning    The Confession
The Reckoning

## OTHER ADULT FICTION

The Postcard

The Crossroad

The Redemption of Sarah Cain

October Song

Sanctuary*

The Sunroom

*www.BeverlyLewis.com*

*with David Lewis

# FROM BEVERLY ... TO YOU

❧   ❧

I'm delighted that you're reading SUMMERHILL SECRETS. Merry Hanson is such a fascinating character—I can't begin to count the times I laughed while writing her humorous scenes. And I must admit, I always cry with her.

Not so long ago, I was Merry's age, growing up in Lancaster County, the home of the Pennsylvania Dutch—my birthplace. My grandma Buchwalter was Mennonite, as were many of my mother's aunts, uncles, and cousins. Some of my school friends were also Mennonite, so my interest and appreciation for the "plain" folk began early.

It is they, the Mennonite and Amish people—farmers, carpenters, blacksmiths, shopkeepers, quiltmakers, teachers, schoolchildren, and bed and breakfast owners—who best assisted me with the research for this series. Even though I have kept their identity private, I am thankful for these wonderfully honest and helpful friends.

If you want to learn more about Rachel Zook and her people, ask for my Amish bibliography when you write. I'll send you the book list along with my latest newsletter. Please include a *self-addressed, stamped envelope* for all correspondence. Thanks!

Beverly Lewis
℅ Bethany House Publishers
11400 Hampshire Ave. S.
Bloomington, MN 55438

# Girls Like You—
# PURSUING OLYMPIC DREAMS!

Don't miss the new series of books from Beverly Lewis called GIRLS ONLY (GO!). In this fun-loving series, you'll meet Olympic hopefuls like Livvy, Jenna, and Heather,

girls training to compete in popular Olympic sports like figure-skating, gymnastics, and ice-dancing. Along the way, they tackle the same kinds of problems and tough choices you do—with friends and family, at school and at home. You'll love cheering on these likable girls as they face life's challenges and triumphs!

## POPULAR WITH SPORTS-MINDED GIRLS EVERYWHERE!

GIRLS ONLY (GO!)
*Dreams on Ice*
*Only the Best*
*A Perfect Match*

Available from your nearest Christian bookstore (800) 991-7747 or from Bethany House Publishers.